PRAISE FOR

THE BLEIBERG PROJECT

"A solid thriller."

—*Publishers Weekly*

"A unique, exceptional thriller… a phenomenon."
—*Gérard Collard, TV host, France 5*

"Khara's thriller, with its pared-down prose, pell-mell pace, and extreme brevity, might remind some of Ian Fleming's Bond novels or Adam Hall's Quiller series…A quick read to be savored as a hurried snack rather than a leisurely French meal."

—*Library Journal*

"This is a great translation, nicely catching the rhythms of US English and developing considerable narrative drive as we quickly get into the action. The narrative is built around multiple flashbacks so we can slowly piece the key events together before and during the War… more interesting than the conventional linear novel."

—*Thinking about Books Blog*

"An astounding thriller."

—*Tele7jours*

"It's fast paced, nonstop action, which makes *The Bleiberg Project* extremely difficult to put down."

—*Smeethsays*

"This book kept me completely involved from the first page. The suspense is incredible because all the events take place in a matter of days. And they are action-packed days. Khara did his research and used it to weave a tale so believable you'll find yourself shuddering because it could be happening right now."

—*Criminal Element*

"This is an excellent thriller that everyone should pick up...another great read from the team at LeFrenchBook."

—*Musing of a Writer and Unabashed Francophile*

"He was this amazing, scarred man who didn't allow himself to have anything other than the work he did and we find out why in *The Bleiberg Project*. That part of the story was riveting. The fight scenes were awesome and jumped off the page when you read them."

—*5-star GoodReads review*

"Khara has written a fast-paced race-against-time thriller with sympathetic characters. Everyone has a secret it seems and it is this vulnerability of each of the main characters that serves as a stark contrast to the power seekers for whom life is cheap...This is a thriller that fans of John Grisham, Robert Ludlum or Ian Fleming will enjoy."

—*The Birch Bark*

"A mix between action movie and an espionage novel, with a tender, human story, all together making it unforgettable."

—*psychovision.net*

"A solid, spellbinding, captivating story that skillfully alternates between fast-paced adventures in the present day and intermissions drawn from history."

"A heart-racing story served up at an exciting pace. The action never lets up, with events piling up at a breakneck pace, leaving the reader barely time to integrate them. The character psychology finely perceived and believable."

The Bleiberg Project

A Consortium Thriller

David Khara

Translated from French by Simon John

LE FRENCH BOOK

First published in France as
Le Projet Bleiberg
by Editions Critic
©2010 Editions Critic

Published by special arrangement with Editions Critic in conjunction with their duly appointed agents
L'Autre agence, Paris and 2 Seas Literary Agency
English translation ©2013 Simon John
First published in English
by Le French Book, Inc., New York

www.lefrenchbook.com

Copyediting by Amy Richards
Cover designed by Melanie Hooyenga at Ink Slinger Designs

ISBNs:
978-1-939474-06-3 (trade paperback)
978-1-939474-89-6 (hardcover)
978-0-9853206-9-0 (Kindle)
978-1-939474-99-5 (epub)

"The farther backward you can look,
the farther forward you are likely to see."
—Winston Churchill

DAY 1

DAY 1

CHAPTER 1

STUTTHOF CONCENTRATION CAMP, 1942.

Two years. Two long years in the frozen hell of northern Poland. You couldn't say he wasn't devoted! Horst Geller had joined the *Schutzstaffel* at the beginning of 1936. He was twenty-three. He had never been a big Hitler fan, but when he saw the way the führer fascinated the mob, he knew joining up was the smart thing to do. Horst had chosen the SS to be left alone, not to be part of Hitler's personal protection squad. As a member of the SS, he knew his family would be respected and protected from the cloud of paranoia that hung over Germany. His homeland had gone insane and taken Europe down with it. But one day, the war would be over, and order would return. Horst was even willing to bet his little apartment on it.

In 1940, he found himself married and soon thereafter, a father. His whole life changed with this double reward. But 1941 hadn't begun well. His higher-ups gave him a promotion, which in itself was good, even if he hadn't asked for anything. But it meant a transfer to Poland to guard a prison camp. It was an important mission, and all of his attempts to refuse the transfer had failed. So Horst had gone, heavy-hearted, leaving his wife, Karin, and his baby daughter, Gisela, behind.

"At least it's not the front," he told his grief-stricken wife in lieu of good-bye. Two colorless summers passed, both followed by winters, proving every night that hell is, indeed, a very cold place. From time to time, Horst got leave and went to Danzig, thirty-five miles to the west, where he'd get drunk and try to forget his solitude with the "soldiers' girls." His pay kept his wife and baby comfortably fed, which meant one worry fewer. Work in the camp wasn't very complicated. He just kept an eye on the dissidents sentenced to forced labor in the *Deutsche Ausrüstungswerke*, a special weapons factory that belonged to the SS. Sometimes he pulled Jews out of trucks and shoved them into the barracks, and once a week he supervised the distribution of the meager rations of bread and turnip soup. He occasionally took pleasure in seeing the Jews in their rightful place, but there were also children, and it was becoming more and more difficult to bear their fearful gazes and pleading. Horst didn't want to hurt them. Of course, he had no sympathy for the Jews, and if he was asked to execute kids, he would, and for a simple reason: It was him or them.

Horst was an ordinary man lost in an endless winter, surrounded by hungry dogs and maniacal executioners. Sometimes he wondered how many other soldiers felt the way he did. How many of the elite soldiers answering to *Reichsführer-SS* Heinrich Himmler wept at night? At least one other, he hoped.

But SS Geller was even more depressed than usual that night. The temperature hovered around five below, and he was standing guard at the hospital, an imposing building much cleaner than the prisoners' barracks. The hospital would have given him the chills if he weren't already frozen stiff. The Jewish children who still had the strength to stand were sent here to satisfy the needs of the strange man who directed the place, known only by the name *Herr Doktor.*

The doctor never left the hospital and never mixed with the guards. Nobody had heard his voice. He communicated his needs in notes to the camp's new commander, Major Hoppe. Sometimes equipment was transferred from the weapons factory to the hospital, but the camp director was the only other person allowed inside. Horst had once come upon Major Hoppe unloading the shipping cases himself. Hoppe was a cruel, brutal man, not the kind of guy to take orders from just anyone, so the doctor had to be an intimidating character. Still, nobody tried to find out more. In the absurd world of Camp Stutthof, ignorance eased one's sleep and extended one's life expectancy.

November 9, 1942, was a special day. That evening, Himmler himself was going to visit the hospital. The camp's best soldiers were told to show the military and spiritual leader of the SS just how impeccably Stutthof was run. If everything went well, Hoppe thought they might receive more resources, men and equipment.

Horst was jittery. He took a long, hard drag on his cigarette and felt the smoke warm him up. His black leather gloves reeked of cold tobacco. He caught sight of a guard with two huge attack dogs patrolling the camp's barbed wire perimeter. At least that guy got to move around.

There were nine soldiers waiting with Horst, conscientiously freezing their asses off in the name of their supreme leader. The group was silent, but the looks they exchanged said much about their general weariness. Himmler and his staff of brownnosers would arrive in a few moments. The men would perform their pantomime without a hitch, and tomorrow morning a hot cup of coffee would help Horst forget the frigid cold.

The evening was bright, and the moon and stars shone from an immaculate sky, lighting up the fine mist that perpetually rose from the region's boggy ground. (The bright yellow searchlights in the guard towers were turned on only in high alerts.) Suddenly Horst and the nine other men threw down their cigarettes and crushed them under their heels. The sound of a motor could be heard coming down the dirt road that connected the camp to civilization. The rumble grew louder. Soon they could make out two approaching military vehicles. To their astonishment, the motorcade had only these two vehicles. The latest news from the front was good, but how could such an important man have such a small escort? Horst concluded the visit was top secret or, at the very least, meant to be discreet. The gates swung open, and the vehicles rolled to a halt in front of the honor guard.

The ten SS men snapped to attention, rifles resting on their left shoulders, their right arms lifted at a forty-five-degree angle, hands extended. Major Hoppe and the doctor hurried down the hospital steps and waited motionless in the middle of the two rows of soldiers. Four blond men emerged from the first vehicle. None were under six feet tall. They wore simple black uniforms in spite of the bitter cold.

One of them moved to the second car, opened its rear door and saluted *Heil Hitler* in a single crisp motion. Heinrich Himmler stepped out and gave the colossal soldier a friendly pat on the arm. A stiff aide-de-camp followed behind, carrying a heavy briefcase. The four men swiftly surrounded the *reichsführer-SS* and his assistant.

Horst watched the spectacle unfold from the corner of his eye. Four Bavarian woodsmen, dressed for August, protecting two little men in glasses, wrapped warmly in their greatcoats. Himmler headed up the two lines of soldiers with his men in tow. Major Hoppe and the doctor tried to hide their disappointment as Himmler momentarily ignored them to review the honor guard, smiling and uttering words of encouragement to the men. Himmler stopped in front of Horst.

"Is this climate too harsh for you, private?"

Surprised, Horst felt his heart begin to race. The devil could read his mind! He seized the opportunity. A little sucking-up couldn't hurt. "For you, Your Excellency, I would guard the North Pole." Himmler came closer. He had the fat, round face of a prosperous family man, but his pince-nez framed a malicious and disturbing expression.

"That isn't what I asked," Himmler replied under his breath. Horst stiffened.

He'd been exposed, but he remained calm. He was tired of pretending. "Poland is hell. I miss Hamburg, Your Excellency."

Keeping his gaze fixed on Horst, Himmler removed his glasses and wiped them clean. "You'll be transferred tomorrow." Horst's smile evaporated, and he swallowed nervously. He'd gone too far. Time stood still. Himmler's face wore a placid expression. "You'll be sent to Wewelsburg Castle. I'm sure you'll find the Westphalian climate more agreeable. I need more people like you—people who speak their minds. I'm surrounded by toadies, competent though they are." He nodded, indicating Major Hoppe.

Horst tightened his salute in relief. "Thank you, Your Excellency." He held back a *Heil Hitler* that wouldn't have helped matters at this point. Himmler turned away and gave instructions as he walked. His assistant nodded in agreement. They joined the camp leaders and swept into the front hall of the top-secret hospital. The masquerade was over.

The other guards gathered around Horst, taking out their cigarettes and lighters in unison. They warmly congratulated their lucky colleague. Horst tried to conceal his happiness, aware that his companions would soon be tormented with jealousy. They eventually dispersed and headed back to their quarters, but Horst stayed alone, his feet planted in the middle of the path. The knowledge that he would soon leave seemed to sharpen his senses. From now on, every breath of this frigid air would bring him closer to Germany and closer to home. He would hate Poland for the rest of his life.

One day he'd forget the horrors committed here. He took out the photo of his wife and baby from his inside pocket and kissed it. Suddenly, his vision blurred. A sharp noise wracked his skull. Where was it coming from? He tilted his head to the right. Orange flames enveloped his shoulder. The cold gave way to warmth, the world teetered, and he fell face-down. As the life painlessly left his body, Horst saw a trickle of blood run across the ground and over the photograph he was still holding in his burned hand. A child's bare feet scampered across frozen earth; this was his last vision. Horst Geller, SS man by happenstance, a husband and father swept up in the general madness of war, died November 9, 1942. He was one of ten official victims in an assassination attempt against Heinrich Himmler. The master of the Black Order survived.

The final solution rolled inexorably onward.

CHAPTER 2

This morning, like every other morning, I'm hung over. My brain is fried. I'm a piece of shit. My head is pounding, and as I grope for aspirin on the bedside table, the lamp falls to the floor and breaks. How did that get there? When I sprinkle two pills into my palm, I feel better already. I toss them back and swallow them dry—water's for pussies. I bury my head in the pillow. I don't know what time it is, and I don't give a damn. There's a nagging sound, like something continually falling—or a lot of little things. My mouth tastes like tobacco. I'm a human ashtray.

I identify the sound. Water. A girl is in my shower. What's her name again? I don't remember, and I don't give a shit either. If she's taking a shower, she's leaving soon. Fine by me. Everything is fine by me, as long as I take the hits. There's one thing left to do, but I don't have the guts. I just want to be done with it once and for all. I could use a rope or jump off a building, but I'm a coward. So until I find an easy way out, I'm killing myself one day at a time. It's the same thing in the end.

She comes through the room, and I open an eye to see what she looks like. Small, brunette, tight. Not bad. She doesn't look at me and probably doesn't know my name either. But now I remember hers. Rachel. Is it Wednesday? Rachel was Tuesday. Actually, no, I don't know her name. She makes an incredible amount of noise for somebody getting dressed. I hear her saying something from the other room. My face is still in the pillow, and I can't understand. Probably "see you later." Sure. See you never.

Finally I'm alone. I open my eyes. The fog in my head is gone, but it took its sweet time leaving. Ten in the morning, and I'm late for work as usual. That bitch splashed water all over the bathroom! I hate that. It's a holdover from the days when I liked everything to be neat and in its place. I mop up the floor with a towel and get in the shower. The warm jets of water massage my body and gradually wake me up.

I'm thirty-one. I'm an asshole trader who works for a piece-of-shit Wall Street firm. I'm just a nobody, but I still seem to have a name: Jay Novacek. I turn off the water and grab a pack of cigarettes that's been left beside the sink. I couldn't just leave it there all alone, poor thing. I light one, because if I'm going to stick with my two-pack-a-day habit I have to get cracking. I look in the mirror and have to admit that I'm pretty well-built, though the memories of college sports and my occasional squash matches seem pretty distant now. I'm a good-looking guy. Girls say so, anyway. Blue eyes and a square jaw—they like that. The mirror steams up, and I can't see myself anymore. Thank God.

10:20. I'm smoking my third cigarette and sprawled on the beige leather couch in the living room. A steaming cup of coffee rests on the glass coffee table. Coffee is the only way I'll make it through the day. If everything goes well, I'll be dressed in ten minutes and in my office before eleven. Miracles can happen.

I hate my apartment. It reeks of money—big, empty and cold. Did I ever like this shit? Leather? Glass and black lacquer? Abstract scribbles and splatters by painters more fashionable than talented? I guess the answer is yes. I recognize my personality only in the plastic Spider-Man and Doctor Doom figurines on top of my stereo system.

I take another drag. I'm a piece of shit who can't even remember what he did last night. But I do remember every detail of one day by heart, to the point that I play it in my mind again and again. How long has it been? Six months? My memory of that day is as vivid as the coffee cup in front of me. I close my eyes and replay the events of that day for the umpteenth time...

I'm at the office. In front of me are six computer screens, blinking everywhere, with graphs, curves, trends, numbers. The world's economy in a nutshell. On the other side of the Earth, people get up, work, pay back their loans, do their best to scrape by. But to me they don't live. They produce. And what they produce makes me rich.

It's Monday morning, and the Dow Jones has collapsed. My friends are all trying to sell, but I'm buying everything that comes past. At the market's close that afternoon, the results are unprecedented: an eleven-point gain. I'm a star. I've just made a billion dollars for my firm, and fifty million of it is mine. Nobody's hotter than me. My boss is on cloud nine. My clients call, one after another, to thank me for what I've done. Champagne in the boardroom with the decrepit senior partners, conservative assholes, every one. The associates join us, and we pass the bottle around. When it's empty we go to dinner—French and expensive. You do what you have to do. The other traders watch us go by like masters of the universe. They throw me dirty looks. They can go screw themselves, the losers. In the elevator we joke and slap each other on the back.

Up until then everything was going fine. The sound of the doorbell snaps me back to the present. 10:23. Shit! Who the hell could it be? Whatever. Go on, asshole, ring all you want. He's a persistent asshole. I drag myself to the door. This apartment is way too big. I slide back the deadbolt and turn the knob. Two huge military men are standing ramrod straight in the hallway. They're wearing their best brass, white gloves, hats, the whole nine yards. Even their medals are out, and these guys have a few. I'd say the first guy, the older one in front, has about fifty. His clone, twenty years younger, has nearly as many. They would seem to serve a purely decorative function.

"Mr. Corbin?" (Nobody's called me that for at least twenty years.)

"Mr. Corbin is my father. I'm Jeremy Novacek."

The penguins don't even flinch. "Jeremy Novacek, we're here to present our sincere condolences on behalf of the armed forces of the United States of America. Your father, Air Force Lieutenant General Daniel J. Corbin, passed away. It's an honor to present you with this flag, as well as your father's military decorations." They give a military salute—rigid but clean. I'm not sure what to do. They don't look like they want to come in and kick back. I salute in return. It seems to work. They turn to the left and leave in step with each other. I push the door shut and stand there. I'm holding a flag folded in a triangle and a box of metal scraps stamped with eagles and stars.

My old man is dead. I lean against the bar in the kitchen, grab a bottle of cognac and throw back a gulp. News like this calls for a celebration. Today's program has just changed: first the office and then a train to Poughkeepsie. I ought to tell my mother that Lieutenant General Corbin finally decided to kick it.

CHAPTER 3

Bernard Dean wore his fifties with elegance. There were no lines on his face, but he was beginning to get moles on his forearms, the first signs of age. His accumulated years only strengthened his character, and the white hair at his temples didn't bother him. He watched the Hudson from the windows of his massive office. As a black man at the head of one of America's most successful financial firms, Bernard was proud of his background. Every day he spent a few minutes of his valuable time reflecting on how he had gotten to where he was and meditating on his success. He was a bold man, perhaps even a bit arrogant. He had overcome his beginnings and had proved to the world that persistence and hard work still had value. Sometimes he wondered if his kind of success would be possible in the future. He wouldn't bet on it. After all, his work was a major cause of unemployment, exclusion and social injustice. But maybe a dedicated black president could kick-start the old kind of American dream Bernard had once believed in.

For the past six months, his morning meditations had been increasingly clouded by his worries for Jeremy. He'd hired brilliant young Jeremy for his dynamism but also for his sensitivity, a rare quality in the world of finance. In a way, Bernard saw himself in Jeremy, who was white, of course, but still—nobody's perfect. They had both grown up without fathers and shared a fierce desire to succeed on their own terms. It took only a week for the two of them to forge bonds that went far deeper than their professional ties. Hypersensitive people tend to be drawn to one another, and with time Bernard had developed fatherly feelings for Jeremy. Maybe he was only filling a hole in his life, but their relationship was sincere. If he had had a son, Bernard Dean would have wanted him to be like Jeremy Novacek. That was why Jeremy's decline weighed so heavily on Bernard, who was frustrated by his inability to ease the young man's suffering. Lately, Jeremy had walled himself off from the world. Still, Bernard kept faith.

As the president of the board at Eckhart, Dean and Aldrin, he clung to the hope that one day peace and forgiveness would finally be granted to both of them.

The phone rang and snapped Bernard out of his daydream. He picked up and hung up without speaking a word. Then he turned back to the windows with his hands behind his back. His office door opened. "Good morning, Jeremy. You're early today. It's not even noon."

"It's a big day. Celebrations are in order." Jeremy's tone shifted. "I have to go to Poughkeepsie to see my mom. I'll be gone a few days."

Bernard turned, expecting to see Jeremy in his usual state of decrepitude. He was astonished to find him wearing an impeccable suit, his face freshly shaven and his hair neatly arranged. He repressed a desire to raise an eyebrow. "Well, look at you, Mr. GQ. To what do we owe the honor?"

"Dad died, and I have to go break the news to Mom."

The news hit Bernard, and his smile vanished. "Well, stay longer than that if you have to. Your mother needs you. She'll be devastated."

"You mean she's crazy."

"Excuse me?"

"It's what the doctors say."

"Your mother is an admirable woman. She's just wrapped up in her worries. Even you can understand that."

Jeremy didn't react. "No, I can't. But now Dad is gone, so at least she'll have a good reason to cry. I'll be back to business as usual in two days max."

Bernard had been calm, but now his face grew rigid with anger. "Listen, Jeremy, stop feeling sorry for yourself for two minutes, and think about it. You have enough money to live comfortably to the end of your days. Get out of here, enjoy what life has to offer, and stop torturing yourself. I'm sick of feeling sorry for you. You think you're the only one with problems? The only guy who feels guilty? Don't expect any more patience from me. You've profited handsomely. Get out of here. Go see your mother, and stay with her as long as it takes. I'll tell security to throw you out if you're back before next week."

The two men stared each other down in silence. Jeremy smiled bitterly and turned to leave. "Whatever you say. You're the boss."

"My patience is wearing thin, Jeremy. If you're trying to get fired, you're on the right track."

Jeremy sucked in his breath. "You can't save me, Bernard. Nobody can. But no matter what you think, I'm glad you tried."

"You're the only one who can pull yourself out of the hole."

Jeremy dropped his head and sighed. "You won't get rid of me that easily," he muttered. Bernard watched him leave. The man he had tried to help was going through hell, and it was, in part, his fault.

CHAPTER 4

The ninety-minute train ride from Grand Central Station to Poughkeepsie seems to last forever. I only go up to St. Francis Hospital once a month. Truth is, I can't bear to see the life slipping out of my mother. The hospital has a good reputation. The doctors and staff are competent and attentive. Mom's been there five years. The Air Force picks up the bill—small compensation for a ten-year stretch with Lieutenant General Corbin. Bernard's right. She's not nuts. She has just let the pain gnaw at her and withdrawn into near-permanent silence. Only my visits bring the power of speech back. But the dialogue never lasts long. Conversations always begin with news of New York, then veer into the career of her little Jeremy. Invariably, the topic of dear daddy Daniel comes up. I pile insults on him. My mother begs me to be more understanding. When the conversation hits the wall, she withdraws into her world once more, and I catch the train back to my pitiful life.

Since what I call deep inside "the fucking accident," of which Mom knows nothing, my visits are fewer and far between. I don't want to turn up a dirty, drunken loser. So I come less often.

Without really knowing how, I find myself in the middle of a long white hallway, outside room 204. A nurse comes out, startling me. "Hey, your mother will be pleased to see you." As soon as she's said it, the young woman takes off down the hallway, a hint of reproach in her eyes.

Before the door closes completely, I grasp the handle and peek inside. Mom's sitting next to the window. She spends her days looking at the gardens inside the hospital compound.

"Hi, Mom." Ann Novacek Corbin turns her head toward me. A smile lights up her wrinkled but shapely oval face. It's not hard to see what a beauty she was. And hard not to be moved by how fragile she is. "Hello, Jeremy, my boy."

I step forward to kiss her. My throat's dry. Tears well in my eyes. I manage to hold them back. A long embrace. Neither of us wants it to end. I wish I could cry, lose myself in her gentle, protective arms and let all my hatred and pain gush out. Become a child again. Return to innocence. But I do none of that. We share an affectionate glance in a silence that Mom breaks. "So, how are you, dear?" I straighten up and shrug.

"In great shape. Don't worry."

"Your suit's a marvelous fit. You always looked good in black. It brings out your beautiful eyes. You have your father's eyes. Did I ever tell you?"

"At least a thousand times, Mom."

I pause. There are a thousand ways to break the news. But faced with the inevitable pain of the loss, none of them seem like the right one. I look down. "Speaking of Dad, I need to tell you something."

"We're not going to fight, are we?"

"No, not today. I brought… Here." I hand her the folded flag and the official letter. She reads it without batting an eye, then folds it and slips it back into the envelope. Only the slight trembling of those parchment hands betrays her grief. They pick at the flag's stars like a cat playing with a blanket. A tears rolls down her cheek. "You're not sad, I suppose."

"No. He walked out on you twenty-five years ago, Mom. He walked out on us. Don't ask me to mourn the guy. At the very most, he was my progenitor. Not my father."

Mom closes her eyes. She mutters a brief prayer. When she opens her eyes again, I flash her a concerned glance. She raises her hands to the nape of her neck and delicately unclasps her necklace. She glides the locket along the long chain she is never without. Her fingers close over the gold medallion. She presses it to her heart, then opens my palm and places in it the most precious thing she has left. The locket infuses me with the warmth of her body. "Here. It's time you knew."

"Knew what? What are you talking about?"

I was expecting wailing, sobbing and a fight like the others we've had so often. Instead, she blindsides me with her locket. "You'll understand one day. Now leave me alone. Come back whenever you want. I'm tired now." She sits in her chair by the window and looks out. I'd waste my breath trying to get another word, the tiniest hint, out of her. I'm rebuffed, dismissed. Despite my curiosity, the blow-off suits me fine. Another minute in this place, and I'll explode. I kiss my mother on her forehead as her gaze wanders once more over the sparse trees in the yard bathed in the soft summer sun.

Dazed, haggard almost, I climb on the Manhattan-bound train, my heart filled with indescribable grief. Sitting on the train, head against the window, I close my eyes and wonder. What did my father die of? Where is he buried? Two crucial things to know, but until now they'd not even occurred me.

Late afternoon. A taxi drops me outside the building overlooking Central Park, at the summit of which I have my luxury penthouse. That evening, I soak longer than usual under the shower. The lump in my throat's been there for hours. I pull on a robe and pour myself a scotch. Drink has become the inevitable salute to a dying day. With night comes intoxication. But not this evening. I set the scotch aside and boil water for tea.

Who am I really? I chew on this for long minutes. Sitting on my couch, I enjoy the tea, looking in the steaming beverage for the solace that relentlessly flees me. Who am I? Jay Novacek—never knew his dad, mom lost her mind years ago? Or Jeremy Corbin, son of a respected senior Air Force officer? Neither answer is correct. The truth—the irrefutable truth—is to be found, as always, between two lies.

When I was a boy, the Corbin family lived in a cozy little house in Hampton, Virginia. Every morning, Daniel Corbin set off for the base, wearing his blue beribboned uniform with sober elegance. And every morning, proud as a peacock, I leaped into Daddy's arms. We had the same buzz-cut blond hair. Then I watched the family Chevy drive away. The rest of the day was spent at school or playing ball. I pointed to every plane that passed overhead. My daddy was flying one of them. Life was the same for lots of kids in the neighborhood. Then, one morning in December 1985, I got up and raced downstairs to kiss Daddy good-bye. And found Mommy crying her eyes out. From that day on, I only kissed a shadow. Adolescence turned sadness into hatred. An engine just like any other to keep going. As soon as I could, I took Mom's name, Novacek. Dad never showed his face again. Now he's dead, twenty-five years after walking out on us. My identity flew the coop and took all the markers I'd laid down with it. Military discipline and values hit the can. I wanted success, money and fast living. Straight A's at Richmond opened the doors to the world of finance. I rose quickly, headed for the holy of holies. Only Wall Street was big enough for my ambition.

Lost in thought, I fiddle with Mom's locket. My fingers glide around its perfect oval rim. A click, and the locket opens, releasing an object that bounces off the beige leather couch and lands at my feet. Cursing, I lean forward and retrieve a small key. I peer at my strange find. The miniscule flat bow of the key is solid and tinted with rust. I delicately scratch it with my nail. The decomposed matter comes away to reveal an engraved motif. I gaze at it. I'm holding in my fingers a key embossed with a swastika.

CHAPTER 5

"Amateurism really jerks my chain. You see, my friend, a hit takes preparation. You watched too many westerns when you were a kid. Cowboys draw, shoot from the hip, and, bam, the baddie's full of holes. In the real world, it doesn't work that way. For example, you didn't take me seriously. You rock up here with a gun in your hand, your ten-gallon hat and your hick boots. You don't study the lay of the land, and, wham, you wonder how come you've got a bullet in your knee. I should be offended, your underestimating me like that. And quit groaning, you're pissing me off." Sitting on a tree stump dampened by the mist hanging over the hillside, the giant pulled a lighter from the pocket of his combat pants. He lit the butt of a cigar taken from his canvas jacket. Beside him lay a camouflage-painted sniper's rifle with a telescopic sight. He scanned the lush, moist Virginia forest.

At the smoker's feet, a man in his early sixties writhed in pain, clutching his left knee with both hands. The red blotch on his gray pants was getting bigger by the second. Judging by the hole and his sorry whining, walking would be a major complication in the future. If he had a future.

"We don't have much time, so if you want to live one day more, let's cut to the chase. Where's the safe, Agent Pettygrow?"

"Jesus, what safe are you talking about? You're crazy, man. You know that, don't you?"

"Your tone is very upsetting. But if you want crazy, you haven't seen anything yet." The cigar-smoking giant ran his hand over his shaven head. Water moistened his palm. He wiped it on his pants and, in a single movement, whipped out a hunting knife with a serrated blade. He hunkered down next to the wounded man and inserted the tip of the blade into his right nostril.

"A swift recap of the situation will help you understand just how deep in the shit you are. One day, for a reason I don't know and don't care to know, you betray your country by selling classified information. You come across a buyer who wants intel on a former Air Force man who's also working for the CIA. You excavate the file and feel your sphincter clench when you realize how sensitive the information is. You don't trust your buyer, and you think that by smoking him just after the transaction, you'll kill two birds with one stone: You keep the money and the secrets. Trouble is, your buyer's even more paranoid than you, and he blows your kneecap away. And now here I am about to cut your nose wide open. Screaming won't stop the pain, by the way. Then I'm gonna slice your eyelids off. This is getting gruesome now. Shall I go on, or have you got the general idea?"

A few minutes later, he had answers to his questions. The bald giant gave the wounded man a friendly pat on his plump, bearded cheek and straightened up. "See, that wasn't hard, was it?"

"Who the hell are you?"

"A guy from far away with a mystery to solve. Far, far away. But if you're keen to know my name, it's Eytan Morg."

The wounded man hauled himself up against the tree stump. The blood gushing from his knee seemed to come straight from his cheeks. He was deathly pale. "That doesn't sound very American."

"Correct. It's Polish. From northeastern Poland, to be precise."

"You work for the commies?"

"Sure! You really are stupid. I work for Mossad, my friend. You realize what that means."

Eyes closed, William Pettygrow recited a silent prayer. Morg slipped his rifle over his shoulder and drew a 9mm pistol with silencer. The execution was swift and painless. The Israeli agent holstered the weapon and dug into an inside pocket. He pulled out a curious object that looked like a hockey puck and placed it on the body. Then Morg doubled back through the woods and headed for the road a hundred yards or so below. Behind the wheel of his pickup, he scanned the trees. A gray cloud wafted out of the forest and disintegrated as it rose into the sky. Having obtained the information he so badly needed, the killer stepped on the gas and was gone.

Later that afternoon, a hunter missed a deer. After an unsuccessful chase, he headed for the tree stump, a marker for all the local hunters. He trudged across a small crater, oblivious to the fact that an administrative operative from Langley had been killed there a few hours earlier. Back in Hampton, the guy stopped off for a beer in a hunters' bar—the only one in the vicinity. To the other regulars he grumbled about his near-miss that afternoon. Close to the sympathetic group, a bald foreigner, taller than any of the other clients, bit into a hamburger and took a slug of Bud. He smiled into his glass. These new explosives really were something else!

Morg hated driving at night on an empty stomach. A quick dessert, one more drink in this rat hole and tomorrow morning, he'd be having breakfast opposite Central Park.

CHAPTER 6

I hang up. Actually, I smash the handset on the base. I have moist palms. My heart's pounding. Any more, and it'll burst through my rib cage. I stuff my keys into the pocket of my jeans. I leave the apartment. The elevator takes me down to the parking garage. What is it, six months since I came down here? At least.

I recoil. The damn light comes on automatically. I perspire. It's hot, but that's not why I'm sweating like a pig. Instinctively, I check my pulse—a tip from the shrink in case of panic attacks. That was before I blew him off. Him and his dumbass way of thinking. Shit, 120 beats a minute. The cars are parked in rows in front of me. I don't live in the projects. The majority are German makes. Porsches are a dime a dozen. To me, it's just scrap metal. Sometimes I miss my beat-up old Beetle. All my friends in college made fun of it, but that car gave me nothing but good memories. OK, where is my car? Surrounded by a hundred or so cars, I take the remote from my pocket. Space 124. OK, I see it now. I see the cover it's hiding under, at least. I'm scared I'll faint. Keep going, Jay. Head up. There are cameras down here. I snap out of it. I'm in front of it now. Gee, it's big. My Aston Martin. I'd forgotten how big it is. I have to pull the cover off. Sweat running in my eyes, my stomach in knots and a lump growing in my throat. No, not that. Close your eyes. Breathe in through your nose, out through your mouth. Visualize the air coming in and going out. Focus on your heartbeat. I'm calm. Calm. Breathe. Nearly there. I wipe my forehead. Now my legs are shaking. Screw it, I can't do it. I can't look at my own car. If this keeps up, I'll never be able to hold the wheel again.

I bang my fist on the bodywork and make a tactical retreat. What the hell was I thinking? I'd forgotten the fear. Excitement and curiosity took me to a place my body isn't ready to go. I have to get to the office, so I'm good for a cab. I turn and stagger toward the door that leads to the elevator. I'm not drunk, but my vision's blurry.

Going up! I give the elevator's glass wall a big hug. Give me some love! And get me out of here fast! Fresh air, at last. Tonight Central Park isn't the lungs of the city. It's my lungs. I like the red brick wall surrounding this section of the park. Tree branches lie on it delicately. When it rains, like now, the leaves trickle water onto the asphalt warmed by the heat of the day. Mist rises, wrapping the neighborhood in a mysterious, almost unreal cocoon.

There's my cab. I'm calm now. I should spend more time outdoors. It does me good. I get lucky. The driver's Haitian but speaks English. "Southward bound, cap'n. Financial district."   No answer. No sense of humor. No surprise.

Back to the big issue. Why did Mom own a key engraved with a swastika? Why'd she give it to me as soon as she found out Dad had died? And what's the rolled-up piece of paper in the locket with… What was written on it again? That's right. UBS LLC 258 2365. I have my own theory about that but nothing definite. At the office I'll have access to the information I need. At this time of night the Asia crew will be in. Nice guys but a real waste of space. They'd be more use stitching Nikes in Malaysia. At least they'd bring in some money.

"You work financial district?" The cabbie brings me back to reality. There's life on his planet.

"No, I want to go jogging under some really tall buildings—in jeans and in the rain."

"All right."

Life but maybe not intelligent life. "I'm kidding. Yes, I work there."

"You no have car?" Jeez, that's a Creole accent.

"No." What the hell does he care? If I take my car, he loses a fare. This isn't good.

He's staring at me in the rearview. I don't like that look. That gleam in his eyes. Has he recognized me? No way. Not six months on.

"I saw you in newspapers last winter." He pulls to the curb. "Get out."

I obey. He doesn't make me pay what's on the meter, pulls away and flips me off. Where am I? A minute or so by foot from Pearl Street. I like this part of Manhattan. Pleasure boats on the Hudson. It feels like a vacation in Key Biscayne. I raise the collar of my leather jacket. Rain trickles down my neck. People hate me. It's to be expected.

In the daytime, this neighborhood is buzzing. At night it's a nuclear winter. Not even a rat ventures out here. Just a few security guards watching building entrances and a handful of cops outside the Fed. Nothing with a pulse. It's ten in the evening, and I'm not drunk. That hasn't happened in an eternity.

At last, the office building. Unbeatable views of the Hudson, the full works, including a heliport on the roof—very practical. The building is staffed twenty-four hours a day, six days a week. I ignore the two doormen watching a baseball game. They glance

blankly at me. They see idiots like me filing past all
day long. I have access to the executive elevator. I run
into no one in the long hallway to the elevators. Stan
Getz accompanies me on my ride to the forty-third
floor. A guy like that plying his talent in an elevator
pisses me off. I step into the empty open-plan office
and wander through a mini-maze. The kingdom of
the telephone, statistics and currency. The history of
the world dematerialized. Sauntering past the Asia
department, I press an ear to the wafer-thin chipboard
wall. Inside, tempers are frayed. Looks like the shit's
hitting the fan in HK or Shanghai. Asian stock ex-
changes are a mess. I laugh. It feels good. I reach my
desk. It looks like a bomb's hit it. Papers everywhere,
magazines, my keyboard buried. The cleanup crew
diligently leaves my clutter as is. I sit down, turn on
the screens and boot up the hard drives.

Out of practice with multi-screen, fighting the
mouse. Online, at last. This isn't garden-variety
Internet. It's the financial whiz kids' network of dedicated servers and sites with confidential information
on bank accounts and movement of capital. From here,
an informed observer can keep an eye on the whole
world's cash flow. I access UBS accounts we deal with.
Nothing. I check to see if the account number appears
in a transaction handled by another firm. LLC 258
2365. Nothing. Jesus, that sequence rings a bell. It's not
an account. An idea, quick.

"If you're looking for a checking account, you're off
track, Jeremy." I nearly jump out of my chair.

"Bernard?" What's he doing here at this time? I relax when I see what he's wearing. "Black tux, bow tie,
white silk scarf. Classy. A few hours of work to come
down from *The Magic Flute*?" He doesn't smile. Before
he would have smiled.

"You think I came here at ten thirty at night to talk male fashion and listen to your jokes?"

In the light of the screens, Bernard looks pretty scary. On his black skin, the red and green reflections give his expression a supernatural tint. "I guess not. So what are you doing here?"

"Security told me you'd shown up. Luckily, I was having dinner nearby."

"How do you know what I'm looking for?"

"For one very good reason, Jay. I hid it."

CHAPTER 7

The coffee's undrinkable—like melted asphalt. Yummy! The waitress pretends to ignore my disgust. The bar brings in the cash during the day, but at 11 p.m. there are few tourists around Battery Park. The Formica tables create a retro-'50s checkerboard. The *American Graffiti* look must wow the foreigners. For me, it's just sordid. I push my cup away. Bernard does likewise. Looking at his face, I figure his thoughts are also wandering in the land of the absurd, the acute awareness of his fancy threads surely playing havoc with his ego.

"OK, can you level with me now? If we're here for the coffee, I have better stuff at home, and so do you."

"The number in your possession corresponds to a safe-deposit box at *Union des Banques Suisses* in Zurich. I arranged for it to be in your name."

I sit up in my turquoise chair. The revelation piques my curiosity. My voice descends to a whisper. "How do you know that I have a safe-deposit box number in my possession? And why did my mother have it? Why the hell did you take out a box in my name?" I breathe out heavily. "Explain. Fast!"

"I will. Reluctantly, but I will. The first time you walked into my office, I thought I was seeing your father. Same walk, same buzz cut, same square jaw. But your eyes had a softness that Daniel always lacked."

I feel sick. "You know my father?"

"He was my best friend at military academy. He'd chosen the Air Force, and I wanted to go into intelligence. At one point, we both wanted to date your mother, but he won out. I saw little Jeremy come into the world. I even carried you to the font when you were baptized. So I guess you could say I knew your father well."

I take my head in both hands, blowing out hard. The operagoer, however, remains imperturbable. "This is nuts! I'm going crazy. You're my boss. You hired me on the strength of my resume. This is totally insane."

"Calm down. You'll get it. It's not too complicated."

"Not complicated? My boss blurts out that he is, in fact, my godfather, wanted to sleep with my mother and knows my father better than I do."

"It's pretty simple."

I can't take any more. "Sure, it's a piece of cake getting on with your life after your dad walks out on you. It's easy watching your mother wasting away with grief. It's easy to have the same nightmares over and over to the point that you're scared of the dark."

"You little jerk. The sun revolves around you, doesn't it? The world's been horrible to you? Screw you! Look at you, selfishly wrapping yourself up in your own misery. I wasn't at the wheel that night. It wasn't me who…"

My chair flies back, and I grab Bernard Dean by the lapel, fist poised to strike. The adrenalin surges through me, tears well in my eyes. I'm like a spring about to let loose. "You old bastard! I'll beat you to a pulp."

He doesn't bat an eye. Calmly wipes the flecks of my spit from his cheeks. The spring snaps. Head slumped, I drown in a flood of tears. I shake from head to foot. I hold my breath and transfer all my energy to my right shoulder. With a beastly, vindictive scream, I punch fast and hard. But all I hit is air. Dean sits there. Just tilts his head a few degrees to his left. His riposte is just as fast. Leaning over the table and off-balance, I feel a hand land on the back of my neck. Big. Broad. Strong.

"If I push now, your nose will paint the table red. It'll give you some real pain to whine about. Now sit down and shut up." The grasp on my neck slackens. I relax. Pick up my chair and sit back down. We stare at each other for a few long seconds. "I'm not sure where to start."

"Start by..." Dean's eyes flash. "OK, I didn't say a word. I'm listening."

"You didn't wind up at our firm by chance. You didn't want to apply, remember? Your mom had to insist. Of course, Ann and I had it planned out since your first day at college. That doesn't make you any less skilled. Your father wanted me to watch out for you."

"You know why he walked out on us, I suppose?"

"Yes. Not the details, but the big picture, yes. He left to protect your mother and you."

"Protect us? Protect us from what?"

"Daniel saw some strange things during a test flight. You must have been five or six years old. He was the kind of guy who had to get to the bottom of things. He investigated and stuck his nose where he shouldn't have. When he realized it, it was too late. We organized a change of identity and had him transferred over to us. Then the Agency placed Ann and you under protection."

"We? The Agency? I don't get it."

"The CIA. I've been a government agent for thirty years. In charge of financial operations. The firm is my cover. In our jargon, I'm what's called a nonoperational agent. Daniel joined the Agency to continue his investigation. I knew nothing about the details of the case. Then a month ago, your father resurfaced and gave me a package that he wanted me to hide away in Switzerland. Your mother gave you the key to that package today, when she found out Daniel was dead."

I don't say a word. The information buzzes in my brain without taking shape, without having any meaning. Through the bar window, I watch cars glide past in the rain. Tires throw up rainbow-colored spray in the neon lights.

"Daniel and Ann never stopped loving each other. And he never stopped loving you. The last time we met, he told me he'd been present at moments in your life without revealing he was there. You were the pride and tragedy of his life."

I return to reality. "Did he know about the accident?"

"No. Nor did Ann. But you know that already."

"He chose an investigation over his own family."

"Were you listening to what I just said? It wasn't an ordinary investigation. It was big. Daniel unsurfaced something from the past, and that made a lot of people nervous. Anyway, nothing's simple at the Agency, and friends can be counted on one hand."

"Do the partners know about your other job?"

"Some, yes. Most, no."

"What am I supposed to do now?"

"It's your call. You have the big picture. Right now your options are limited. Either you know enough, or you need to dig for more. I think I can guess which way you're going to go."

Dean glances at his watch. "It's midnight, and you're not drunk. That's encouraging." His tone wasn't mocking.

"I don't feel like drinking. Why are you telling me all this tonight? Why not before? Or never?"

"Before? I'd promised not to. Never? That was the plan. But the situation's changed."

"Daniel J. Corbin is dead."

"Yes. And that makes me immensely sad. But we have to concentrate on the living. I don't understand why the army sent people to your apartment. Your dad was no longer Air Force, so they had no business even knowing about his death. You should not have been contacted."

"So?"

"It means Daniel's cover was blown. And that's not good, Jeremy. Not good at all."

CHAPTER 8

It's one in the morning when Bernard drops me outside my building. The rain's stopped. Pity. My head's
pounding, but I haven't touched a drop of booze all
evening. To celebrate I find myself caught up in something way over my head. Bernard's big sedan roars
away. He gestures with his hand. If he's not waving
good-bye, it means he's either picking wax out of his
ear, or he wants me to call him tomorrow. I will. I
zip up my jacket all the way. I don't want to sleep. I
wander around the park, hands stuffed in my pockets. What a day! Crying helped. The shrink was right.
Yelling and smashing are highly therapeutic. Now
what? My father's dead. From grade-A asshole, he's
achieved some kind of hero status. My mother knew
and didn't say a word for over twenty years, and now
she hands me a Swiss safe-deposit box number and
a key with a pretty little swastika on it hidden in a
locket. My boss, the only guy that I can remotely call
a friend, tells me he's known me forever and works for
the CIA. No doubt about it, one hell of a day. I ask
myself again—what now?

Bernard's smart. He sensed curiosity overwhelming me. He knows I have no choice. I'm catching that
plane to Switzerland to pick up the parcel my father
left for me. I have to get to the bottom of this. Take
a shaker. Add a shot of Air Force, a slug of CIA, two
fingers of Switzerland and a twist of Nazi. That's a

cocktail I can't resist. I have a passport, cash and time on my hands. I have no other appointments to keep. Leaving the country awhile won't do me any harm. Bernard will go with me. I'd bet my life on it.

I'm outside the Guggenheim. Some Japanese tourists are snapping pictures. You have to admit, a cylindrical building, only in New York. The tourists make me laugh. But I'm no better than them. I live a few blocks away, and I've never set foot in the place. There was a time when I liked art. There was a time.

I double back. My bed's calling. Strange, it's the middle of the night, and I still don't want a drink. On the other hand, I'm not about to quit smoking. I toss my now-empty second pack for the day in the trash and open up my third pack. I wonder about the big secret the old man stumbled across. What makes a man walk away from his family and vanish? My belly rumbles. I'm not thirsty, but I am hungry. I haven't swallowed anything solid since yesterday. A sandwich and candy bar hit the spot. A smoke, food—life doesn't seem so bad. It's sad to say, but it's taken my dad's death for me to feel alive for the first time this whole damn year.

§ § §

Eytan Morg dropped his keys into the hotel valet's palm. The guy stared in amazement. At the Four Seasons, a muddy pickup got a bigger reaction than a Ferrari. The giant smiled at the valet's slack-jawed expression. Among the perks of his profession was a hefty expense account. Other agents stayed in sleazy motels and faked invoices to stash money away. He preferred to treat himself. Money would come and go. There were bigger things to worry about. And statistically, it was more likely that you'd be shot in a cheap dive downtown than in a five-star luxury hotel. Morg stopped in his tracks, dropping his green canvas sports bag on the floor at his feet. Hands on hips, he let out a long whistle that earned him some suspicious glances.

Moody lighting, walls in shades of beige, huge red porcelain vases, marble floor. Classy! He had stopped beside a glass display case holding three diamond necklaces—the work of a French jeweler at the peak of his career. The prices were discreetly hidden. Another display showcased the talents of Swiss watchmakers. Morg scanned the pieces on offer with a connoisseur's eye.

A man in his forties and a three-piece suit came around the reception desk to intercept the intruder. He cleared his throat to interrupt the window shopping. "Perhaps I can help you, sir?" Morg adored obsequiousness. He peered down at the man, who was a good ten inches shorter.

"Sir has a reservation. Sir is awed by the beauty of the place. And sir's name is Eytan." He thrust out a virile hand and cracked a big smile. "And you are?"

"Er, Friedkin. James Friedkin. I'm the night manager, sir."

"Tsk-tsk. Eytan."

"Yes. Eytan. Would you care to step to my desk to check in?"

"With pleasure, James."

A few minutes and some fastidious formalities later, the night manager ushered his guest into a studio suite. Morg glanced appreciatively at the king-size bed and the living area separated from the sleeping area by a brown velvet couch. Above all, he was blown away by the floor-to-ceiling windows offering an unbeatable view of the Manhattan skyline.

A bellhop, slightly awkward in his old-fashioned red uniform, arrived with a black case, which he handed to James before snapping to attention.

"Sir, your assistant left this case for you yesterday," James said to Morg. "As per your instructions, we kept it in the vault until you arrived."

"Fine, James. Thank you very much for your warm welcome. Now, if you don't mind, I'd like to..." He nodded toward the door.

"Of course, sir... er, Eytan. Enjoy your stay. Don't hesitate to ask if you need anything." In a flash, the two hotel employees were in the hallway, hundred-dollar bills in their hands. They chatted briefly about this strange but friendly guest before going back to their duties.

Morg grabbed the case and settled down on the couch. No opening mechanism was visible. Another innovation from the guys at R&D. He positioned his thumbs on the sides of the handle and heard a slight click. The top half of the case swung up, revealing the precious contents. Morg reached for the two magazines first and slipped them into his jacket pockets. Then he took out a brown paper envelope, which held a tidy sum of cash, half American bills, half euros. He guessed it was at least twenty grand. Working for Mossad brought little thrills like this. A second envelope held a series of pictures of a blond guy with a buzz cut, the kind of player who'd spend more time in front of the bathroom mirror than in the library. The detailed description revealed that blondie was thirty-one and a financial whiz in a booming Wall Street firm. Bachelor, no kids. Unfortunately for him, he had no military training. Finally and most important, Morg looked at the assignment codes. Two applied to this Jeremy Corbin guy: 111a and 111b. The first, surveillance, was hardly surprising. It was the second that elicited a heavy sigh from Agent Morg. Grumbling, he drew his gun and checked the clip.

§ § §

At the same time in Poughkeepsie, the night nurses at Saint Francis Hospital were preparing the patients' morning medications. The two nurses swapped raunchy remarks about the new oncologist, whose model good looks would make an appetizing afternoon snack in the storeroom. They continued discussing their not entirely implausible fantasy as they left the room. In the hallway, a colleague with short red hair and an athletic build passed by and nodded to them. She was a few inches shy of six feet, with a pale, angular face and small brown eyes that lent it a cruel expression.

The two friends were too busy laughing to see her swing into the room they had just left.

§ § §

The girls are burning it up on the dance floor. Rapid-cut videos play on two huge screens. My skull's pounding with the heavy bass. The seething mass in the stroboscopes is whooping and shouting. The only guy in the whole firm not suffering from arthritis, I launch myself into the crowd, arms up high. I'm soon surrounded by a clutch of diabolically sexy babes in miniskirts.

Bodies touch, then rub together, forming a heaving and sensual whole. The music makes the debauchery all right. High-class hookers have moved in on my bosses. They can afford them, but tonight is on me. It's my day. Money, power, women. We are masters of the universe in a gloriously pathetic caricature. Who cares? Morality, codes of conduct and good behavior are for losers. The chick with her tongue down my throat wouldn't look at me twice if I were a mechanic or steelworker. Her friend wouldn't be copping a feel if I didn't drive an Aston Martin. And I'm going to sleep with them both because I'm rich. They say power is a great aphrodisiac. It's true. Vile but true. I'm about to prove it. One last flaming scotch with the new loves of my life. A great shot of alcoholic vapor in the nostrils. Bartenders call it a shooter. It certainly kills you.

No point saying good-bye. Everybody's in good hands. These aren't women on my arms, but two crutches helping me walk straight. The valet brings up my DB9. However hard I look, only James Bond's wheels suit my present and future standing. And away we go for a high-speed ride through downtown Manhattan. Let's enjoy the moment.

The blonde chick puts her heels on the walnut dash. That makes me mad. I knock her feet away and start to explain with a stern bordering-on-crude lecture that you don't behave like that in a car that's worth more than her whole apartment. Suddenly, two screams ring out. I'm propelled toward the wheel, but the airbag stops me. I screech to a halt and leap out like a wildcat. A couple stares at me in disbelief. Lying on the pavement a dozen yards away is an upside-down stroller. Blood trickles out of it.

My father was taken from me. I've just taken a child. I slump down on the sidewalk and begin to retch.

I puke my guts out on the pavement and try to get my head around what I've done. I wipe my mouth with the lapel of my jacket. I pull out my state-of-the-art cell phone. "Bernard, I've screwed up."

"Tell me where you are. I'm on my way."

I tell him. I hurl the damn phone against the wall. The hookers have melted away. The parents are in tears, kneeling over the stroller. They speak a language I don't know. The father points at me. They look like the Al-Qaeda people you see on TV. His swarthy complexion and black beard close in on me fast. He hits me. He's going to kill me. That's fine. I killed his four-month-old daughter.

This day was supposed to be mine.

That's when I always wake up. I'm condemned to re-live the scene every night. And the shrink asks why I can't sleep.

DAY 2

CHAPTER 9

The English doctors had done a remarkable job. The crash landing wasn't part of the plan. The broken ankle either. Another three weeks' rest, and he'd be gamboling around Berlin. No doubt the führer would be proud of him and the risks he'd taken for the grandeur of the Reich. Even Himmler and Göring would stop shouting their mouths off. For months, he'd suffered the humiliations in silence—excluded from crucial meetings, sidelined from decisions about the war. But this mission was his and his alone. And he was going to change the course of history.

The unhappy child, bullied by a controlling father who had moved the family to Egypt for business reasons, wasn't doing so bad. He'd developed a taste for insubordination from an early age, but only when he was twenty-one and the Great War was raging did he rebel against his father's strictures, abandoning his boring business school to enlist in the hope of becoming a fighter pilot. The war ended before he could join the battle for the sky, but at least he'd broken free of his oppressive family. Then came the move into politics and the decisive encounter with Adolf Hitler. Together, the two men rose through the ranks of the National Socialist German Workers' Party. After the failed

Beer Hall Putsch in 1923, they were incarcerated in Landsberg Prison, Bavaria. For eight long months, Hitler dictated to him what was to become the foundation of the new world order, *Mein Kampf.* The Nazis' hour of glory lay on the horizon. Rudolf Hess's had already passed.

The sound of a key turning in the lock brought him back to the present. The cell door opened. Douglas Douglas-Hamilton, the fourteenth duke of Hamilton, ducked his head to enter the room. The architects of the Tower of London had not designed the building for lanky aristocrats. The prisoner examined his visitor. Six feet six inches tall, slim and perfectly nondescript. In his tweed suit, he looked like a giant green bean. To Rudolf, he was the caricature of a British lord: crooked teeth, hair flopping over his forehead, long nose. In short, the duke was the epitome of ugliness.

Once he was through the door, Hamilton straightened up, thrust his hand out and pumped the prisoner's hand. He glanced around and found the room on the comfortable side. A cozy bed next to a chair and a desk covered with newspapers. Multicolored vials were lined up on the window ledge. Very German. "My dear Rudolf, I'm very pleased to see you being so well treated. Forgive the amateur dramatics, but in the present circumstances it's important to make people think you're being incarcerated."

Standing up with some pain, the Nazi pulled over the chair and sat down. "My lord, it's a pleasure for me, as well. MI6 explained the necessity of this masquerade. It suits me perfectly. I won't be a difficult guest. Once our agreement is finalized, and I have been released, I'll take advantage of my stay in your fine country to visit Oxford. My father wanted me to study there."

Hamilton let out a stiff chuckle, which he concealed behind an awkward cough. "I shall be your guide. I spent lovely years there. How are you? Our last meeting dates back to the Olympic Games, I believe."

"True. We shared breakfast in your hotel in central Berlin. I won't lie. I'm impatient to return home. My ankle is on the mend. Other than that, I'm as well as can be."

The Scotsman admired the German's flawless diction with no trace of accent. But the duke had more important things on his mind than the Nazi leader's diction. At the duke's request, a guard discreetly brought in a second chair. His task accomplished, the man left, locking the door behind him. "Herr Hess, now that we are alone, let's get down to business, shall we?"

"With pleasure. Peace between our two nations is a pressing issue. Thanks to the prospect of our forthcoming treaty, an invasion of the Russian front is imminent. Our army is massing its troops to attack the Bolsheviks, to the delight, I should imagine, of the Americans and Mr. Churchill."

"Excellent news! We have no wish to see Stalin become a major player on the world stage."

"We'll ensure he doesn't. Have faith in the führer's strategic genius. In a few weeks, the support of your air force will guarantee us a crushing victory. We shall celebrate Christmas in Moscow." In his excitement, Rudolf pummeled his good knee with his fist.

"God willing," Hamilton replied with a wolfish grin.

"And as good things always come in pairs, I should tell you that one of our scientists has obtained some very promising results."

The duke's eyes opened so wide, they threatened to pop out of their sockets. His face was a picture of pure covetousness.

"His latest experiments seem to confirm every hypothesis," Rudolf Hess continued smugly. "Ours and yours. There is, of course, still work to be done, but we're on the right track."

The duke nibbled his lower lip. He could hardly conceal his eagerness, but his upbringing reasserted itself, and he restrained himself. "Radiation might work, then? What does your expert say? Remind me of his name again."

"Bleiberg. Professor Viktor Bleiberg. He is enthusiastic, as you can imagine. But he is a man of science and constantly demands more tests and more guinea pigs. Thank goodness we're not short of subjects to experiment on." The Nazi's smile faded when he saw the duke's stern expression.

Hamilton cleared his throat. "Bleiberg? I confess I'm somewhat surprised. The name sounds Jewish."

"Indeed. But you must remember, my dear Hamilton, that as this project is ultimately my responsibility, I decide who is Jewish and who isn't." Hess looked offended. It was a pretense. In reality, the project was Himmler's. In the power game being played out in Berlin, Hess's grasp of strategy had proved sadly deficient. Hitler's official deputy had soon found himself relegated to third place in the regime behind the unbearably duplicitous megalomaniac Göring. And now Hitler swore only by Himmler.

The entrance of an insignificant man in a tight-fitting gray suit jerked the Nazi out of his thoughts. The man bowed slightly to the duke and gave him a brown leather briefcase. Hamilton extracted a thick file. Taking the briefcase with him, the messenger exited, shutting the two men in together once more.

"Let's see, as far as the Jews are concerned, do as you please. You are the masters of continental Europe. But if you have no objection, I would like us to go through Herr Hitler's proposed treaty together. Churchill will sign it as soon as I give my approval."

"It will be a pleasure. I can't wait to put an end to this sham imprisonment and move into more comfortable accommodations."

The examination of the treaty setting out the conditions for peace between Britain and Germany took many hours. Hess's enthusiasm was a contrast to the duke's stoicism. *The English are quite inscrutable*, mused Hitler's emissary.

"Excellent. I have an appointment with the prime minister this evening, and I think things will move fast. To be absolutely thorough, there is one point that needs clearing up. If everything goes as planned, I shall look forward to taking you to the opera next week."

The German's face lit up. His bushy eyebrows twitched at the mention of classical music. "With pleasure. I'm touched that you should remember how much I love opera."

"Don't mention it, truly. Let's try to conclude, shall we? My last question concerns the antidote. Do you have the formula with you?"

"Antidote is not the right word. Rather than reverse the effects of the radiation, the solution apparently allows the cells to avoid necrosis. Bleiberg is very particular about the nuance. Scientists, you know." Hess's jocular tone elicited no response. The endless hours of discussion appeared to have gotten the better of Hamilton's good nature. Hess cleared his throat and reached toward the pile of books on the floor next to his bed. He opened a fine edition of *Hamlet* and took out a carefully folded piece of paper, which he handed to the duke.

"Here. I learned the elements by heart without understanding a single line. That's how secrets are spread. I jotted down the formulas and the ingredients." Hess thought he saw a slight trembling of the aristocrat's hand when he took the piece of paper. Without a word, Hamilton tucked it into the breast pocket of his jacket and knocked on the door. As it swung open, he reached out to shake the German emissary's hand.

"Herr Hess, I am very grateful, on behalf of my organization, for your devotion. I'll keep you informed as soon as I receive further instructions." A warm glow spread across the Nazi's cheeks. He'd done it! No nation could counter a British-German axis. Moreover, humanity was about to experience its most significant evolution. All thanks to him. Their handshake was virile. Hamilton left the cell, and the door swung closed. Then the slot in the door opened. The duke's large head appeared in its frame. Gripped by sudden anxiety, Hess hobbled over.

"Oh, it completely slipped my mind, but I fear I shan't be able to take you to the opera after all."

"Why so?" The anxiety deepened.

"You see, Rudolf, Churchill has absolutely no intention of signing any agreement with Hitler. In fact, we hope to convince America to join the conflict shortly. We trust the arrogance of your Japanese friends will help us persuade Uncle Sam."

"What? But you said…"

"Tsk-tsk, Rudolf. A grown man like you shouldn't allow himself to be taken in. I see now how Himmler succeeded in overtaking you in the führer's affections."

"You knew?" seethed Hess. Panic turned to rage.

"Naturally. MI6 isn't staffed by no-hopers. What's more, we have informed Hitler that you were carrying a draft peace treaty, and he has denied all knowledge of your plan. He has completely dissociated himself from your initiative."

"But he..." Hess' voice trailed off as thoughts swirled in his brain.

Hamilton stepped back from the opening. "Your case looks pretty hopeless, I fear. And now that I have this," the duke said, patting his breast pocket, "along with the name of the scientist in charge of the Big Project, you serve no purpose. I am sincerely sorry."

Hess stared at the floor in despair. He shook his head incredulously.

"We will make contact with this Bleiberg chap," Hamilton went on. "As for you, as of today, you are no longer in full possession of your mental faculties. Can you imagine the beauty of it? The louder you protest, the more apparent your madness will be to the whole world. You will be tried after the war and will rot in jail. We'll make sure of that. By the way, I'm not the duke of Hamilton. My poor fellow, your naivety is quite pitiful."

Rudolf lunged at the door, screaming in a mix of German and English. "Bastard! You have no right! *Sie sind verrückt!* Curse you and your consortium! The führer will raze your cesspit of an island. You'll die under our bombs, and our panzers will flatten the last vestiges of your decadent civilization!" The phony Hamilton smiled and closed the slot. The muffled hammering of fists on steel echoed down the hallway. Soon, there was nobody there to hear.

Rudolf Hess was secreted away in a British jail until the end of the war. In 1946, at the Nuremberg trial, he argued that he had attempted to bring the war to an early end by offering Britain an alliance with Germany. He was sentenced to life in prison for conspiracy and crimes against peace. Hess became prisoner No. 7 in Spandau prison, West Berlin. He remained locked up until August 17, 1987, when his guards found him hanging in his cell. He was nine-ty-three years old.

He filled many notebooks during his captivity. They were all burned.

CHAPTER 10

As he did most mornings, Eytan watched the sun rise. It would be a warm, sunny day. Summer was on its way. He prayed that his mission would be over before the thermometer soared into the high eighties. The walkways in the park were already swarming with tourists of every color, language and origin. He knew of no other place that so deserved the name melting pot. It didn't displease him. He genuinely enjoyed observing humanity. He had worried that constant killing would deprive him of part of his own humanity, but in fact the job gave him a greater sense of accomplishment than loss. A cup of cappuccino in hand, he watched the entrance to Corbin's building. Eytan's steely gaze scanned the street while he replayed the events of the previous weeks in his mind. He was convinced of one thing: The denouement of this affair was approaching. At last.

The possibility that his "client" had already been eliminated crossed his mind. He promptly dismissed it, figuring that he was a good half day ahead of the invisible enemy he had been playing cat-and-mouse with for the last few months. Three hours spent leaning against the park wall had led the agent to two conclusions. First, the neighborhood was populated by the extravagantly wealthy. If a killer wanted to slip unnoticed into any of its buildings, the dress code was suit and tie. Second, the target was not the kind of guy to head off for work at dawn. So Eytan wait-ed. Patience was an integral part of his job. Luckily, there was something handy to read. Eytan dug into his pockets for some change and fed it into one of the colorful newspaper boxes vying for his attention. He chose *The New York Times*, to his eyes the most author-itative of the papers on offer. The layout was appalling. Only an American could understand this mishmash of headlines, columns and words. But what did they say? No pain, no gain.

As ever, the news encapsulated a world in chaos. The economic debacle had engendered a cultural crisis. The measured optimism of the global stock markets glossed over the beating the great unwashed were tak-ing—unemployment, rampant poverty, evictions.

These reporters seemed to be rediscovering scourges that had afflicted the underclass since the dawn of time, well before the advent of financial chicanery. Nothing new there. NBA and NFL franchises were busy trad-ing players, but Eytan skimmed over the sports pages. In the Middle East, the situation remained unstable. In Africa, the West continued to plunder resources—a gi-gantic new oil field had been discovered. In the United States, Medicare reform was once more the big issue.

There was a health scare in Mexico. An especially deadly influenza virus, according to the *Times*. Local and international organizations, under the supervision of the World Health Organization, had established quarantine procedures to isolate blah blah blah. Eytan smiled. It's awesome how you can feed people the same old bullshit time and again without them notic-ing. In three months, face masks would be everywhere, pharmaceutical firms would be selling millions of doses of a miracle vaccine to overanxious or corrupt governments...

After going through three sections with one eye on the news and the other on Corbin's building, he felt like he was getting a permanent squint. The paper joined the remains of his breakfast in a nearby trashcan. Around ten, the sidewalks and streets began to busy up. Long-distance surveillance became tricky. Eytan considered crossing but had no desire to wind up a pancake on the blacktop.

While waiting for the walk sign at the nearest crossing, Eytan noticed a black Chrysler limo pulling up outside the building. The limo didn't stand out in any way in this upscale neighborhood. It was the tags that attracted Eytan's attention—pale blue with a curved red band at the top and "Diplomat" clearly printed on them. Eytan memorized the number: D PR08-68 UN. He racked his brains. D for Diplomat, obviously. UN for the United Nations, simple. But he felt a growing sense of foreboding. Shit, what did PR stand for again?

The traffic stopped. Pedestrians crossed. Two bulky guys got out of the limo, which immediately merged back into traffic. Eytan walked faster, then broke into a sprint as the guys entered the building.

PR. The country code for Argentina.

§ § §

Crucial discovery: I can sleep without getting wasted the night before. Now that's encouraging news. Bernard shook me up last night, but can I blame him? I'm caught up in something straight out of an Ian Fleming novel.

Considering the circumstances, I'm shocked to realize that the events of last night have left me feeling great, like I've awakened from a long sleep, shucking off my torpor and stepping back into reality. But which reality? I'm confused, which is only natural. The trip to Switzerland will provide the key to this whole strange business. I'll drop by the hospital to give Mom a hug before I leave. I owe her that, at least.

The phone rings. I get up. Weird. Something's wrong. The walls are straight, the floor's flat. I'm not staggering. I was almost used to lurching instead of walking. In a straight line, the phone's not so far. I pick up. A woman's voice asks if I'm Jay Novacek. I nearly blow her off. I'm Jeremy Corbin. But I'm not sure the name's very safe. So I say yes. She talks. The more she says, the less I understand. The handset slips from my grasp. My knees buckle. I crumple to the floor. I rewind the words. "I'm very sorry to tell you your mother died this morning from a heart attack. My sincere condolences. Could you drop by today to take care of some administrative matters?"

I thought it would take longer for my world to collapse. My father, then my mother. The earthquake starts in my gut, and soon I'm trembling from head to foot. Tears erupt from my eyes. I want to trash the whole place, demolish the walls with my bare fists. A second later, I'm sobbing, sprawled on the rug. The pain is massive and overwhelming. Not her, not now.

Suddenly, it hits me. I'm next.

My cell phone vibrates. Startled, I grab it without thinking. It's Bernard. "Bernard, Mom's…"

"I know. We have to act fast. You're in danger. Do exactly what I say." He talks, I listen. I sense he's scared. I'm scared, too. Now I'm not sure I want to croak anymore. At least not before I've gotten to the bottom of all this. Not before I get payback.

I skip the shower and get dressed fast. I stuff random clothes into my black leather travel bag. Passport in pocket, I throw on a jacket, pull my Yankees hat down low and head out. Following Bernard's instructions, I bypass the elevator and take the stairs. Cigarette dangling, I race down them. Twelve flights at this speed will soon tone up those calves. I glance at my watch. Ten in the morning. I nearly slip on the thick red carpet that the building's interior designer felt obliged to put in the lobby. Looks good, but it's gonna kill someone one day.

I glance down. A guy's running up the stairs. Black suit, shades, buzz cut—the full *Men in Black* outfit. I get a nasty feeling about the guy. I double back, heading for my floor. Look up. Jesus, another guy—the first guy's clone—is coming down. I'm trapped. No time to think. My only chance is the fire escape. Nobody's going to save me. It won't happen. The building's full of money grubbers. At this time of day, they're already at their desks. Through a door, down a hallway. Running. The two undertakers can't be far behind. In under five seconds, I'm at the window.

Shit! A third hit man has this base covered. He's coming in. And like an idiot, I'm headed straight for him. I'm screwed. Weirdly, he's not dressed like his buddies. They're channeling the prez's Secret Service operatives. He's straight out of the woods, in combat pants and jacket, lumberjack boots, green long-sleeve crew-neck shirt and no shades. He's as bald as a coot and has to be at least six-feet-six. I don't like the look on his face, but I can admire the smooth way he draws two guns equipped with silencers.

I look him straight in the eye, but it's like he sees through me. He takes off feet first and whacks me in the belly with his size 14's. Winded, I fall on my butt.

I've been getting too friendly with the floor lately. Two muffled bangs. Then two more. It's good to know dying doesn't hurt. Woozy, I lower my head to check out the holes in my stomach. No blood.

The bald guy's flat-out facing me, guns outstretched, eyes focused on something over my head. Four cartridges bounce and roll on the carpet. I turn my head to see what's behind me. The two goons are sprawled face-down. I spin back around to see the giant's reaction. Without using his arms, he flips back onto his feet. Very impressive. The guy seems almost laid back. He holds out a paw the size of Michael Jordan's. I grasp it and haul myself up with a lot less grace. "Who are you?" It's as good a question as any.

"You don't recognize me?" he asks in surprise. I think. Nothing comes to mind.

"No. Should I?" It's as good an answer as any.

"I'm your best friend." Yul Brynner grins and clocks me. Back on my butt. But this time he's punched my lights out.

CHAPTER 11

Bernard Dean was in a foul mood. In the last twenty-four hours, he'd received more bad news than in all his thirty years of active service. Daniel Corbin's death was not a good sign. Ann's death was tragic proof of that. Added to these personal losses, a liaison officer from Langley, William Pettygrow, had gone missing. Pettygrow's unit had access to the details of every agent who needed a change of identity. A quick check confirmed Dean's hunch—Pettygrow handled Corbin's file. The reason for the soldiers' little visit to Jeremy to announce his father's death was simple. The twenty-year-old secret was out. All Dean had to find out now was who benefitted and why. The Swiss safe-deposit box, the key Ann kept—it was all part of an obscure and sinister puzzle.

Dean thought back to the call he had taken five minutes earlier. The conversation disturbed him even more. Knowing that the call came from an undetectable encrypted cell phone didn't help. But that voice echoed like a distant memory. They'd met. He'd bet his life on it. Fingers clenched on the wheel of his sedan, Dean was speeding through heavy traffic toward Central Park. It took him a good quarter hour to reach Jeremy's building. He parked and reached into the glove box for his small-caliber pistol, which he kept in his hand, concealed under his coat. At times like this, you couldn't be too careful.

Glancing left and right, he reached the entrance in a few strides. Following the Agency's playbook to the letter, Dean ignored the elevator and took the stairs. In the absence of anybody else, friend or foe, on the staircase, he cursed his age as he climbed the steps. His lungs burned, and his thighs would be aching all day. His stamina was waning, but he still had surprising physical strength on his side and solid experience. The term "nonoperational agent" was never more appropriate, but aging provoked no existential angst for Dean. What it provoked was just one crucial question: If the anonymous phone call was a trap, would he be able to defend himself?

He was still expecting to find out when he arrived outside Jeremy's apartment, scanning the hallway and peering at the small wall lamps on either side of the elevator. Imitation gold lampshades—an ode to banality of the kind a good agent couldn't resist. As per his telephone instructions, Dean examined the lamp on the left, running his fingers over it. Behind the lamp socket, he felt a mushy lump and a key. After several attempts, he pulled out the key and, to his disgust, the blob of freshly chewed gum with which his mysterious informer had stuck it in place. Gross-out schoolboy humor, he thought.

Dean dropped the gum to the floor, pressed his ear to the wall next to the door and listened. Silence inside the bachelor pad. Noiselessly, he opened the door and entered a living room whose owner clearly had a very loose grip on the concept of cleanliness. The remains of a snack were scattered across a large glass coffee table. The closed shutters over the floor-to-ceiling windows allowed only a little light in. Tall speakers dominated the four corners of the room. A state-of-the-art hi-fi and plasma TV adorned the wall to Dean's right. Fifties jazz posters hung along-side modern art. A battalion of empty bottles stood in rows on the floor near the beige leather couch. A glass ashtray overflowed with cigarette butts. More were scattered on the rug. If the living room had been designed for conviviality, it had been transformed into an altar to despair and self-neglect. The reek of cold tobacco tickled Dean's throat.

The CIA veteran walked down the short hallway to the bedroom. Through the open door, he glimpsed the foot of the bed. And on it, Jeremy's feet.

§ § §

As laid-back as ever, Eytan sauntered across the ho-tel lobby. After one night in the place, he was known to absolutely everybody. For a secret agent, a high profile is the best way to go unnoticed, he joked to himself, even if he didn't feel much like laughing. When a Metsada agent came across a car with Argentinean diplomatic plates, he had every reason to worry. Since the 1950s, the country had been home base for a whole bunch of Nazi fugitives and not just the small fry. At least he had eliminated two guys whose intentions were anything but amicable.

But the true cause of Eytan's bad mood was his encounter with Corbin. This surveillance assignment would only be trickier now that the chump had seen his face. The Israeli hit man had been forced to act, but the consequences discretion-wise were disastrous. That encounter changed everything. The call to Bernard Dean was one more complication, but he had to make sure Corbin would be in safe hands. Eytan never expected to cross paths with the CIA veteran again. In some respect, it was the only good thing that had happened all day.

Eytan entered his suite, discarded his combat jacket and shirt on the king-size bed and opened the high-tech case that had been left for him at the hotel reception desk.

CHAPTER 12

"Don't take this the wrong way, sir, but are you sure there's no alternative?" The young woman frowned with a combination of irritation and apprehension. "Jacqueline, ordinarily your insubordination amuses me, but not today. Please, don't make me pull rank on you." Bernard Dean couldn't lose his temper with Jackie Walls. Any other agent would have felt the full force of his anger by now. The small blonde had always managed to wrap him round her little finger. He knew it, and usually it amused him.

"Sir, I'm no expert in witness protection. I don't mean to disobey orders. It's just that I'm scared I'll disappoint you."

"Barbie," as her coworkers at Langley called her, was infuriatingly stubborn and surprisingly self-deprecating. "Jackie, save that for someone who's never seen you at work."

Her bright, innocent smile emphasized the roundness of her cute face. "Oh yes, silly me. I can't fool the man who trained me." She put on a perfect mock-contrite pout.

There, she'd done it again. Unable to resist, Dean rolled his eyes. "And for the last time, lose the pigtails. You look ridiculous."

"If you read the women's magazines, sir, you'd know that pigtails are in this summer," protested Jackie.

Dean nodded toward the bathroom door. Grumbling, she headed for it.

Dean leaned over Jeremy, who was painfully opening his eyes.

§ § §

A major scoop! St. Peter is black. And he's looking at me with a worried expression. It's not St. Peter; it's Bernard. I must be alive. Apparently I can turn my head. Move my toes. And hands. But my hooter's killing me. A quick glance tells me I'm in my bedroom, on my bed. What am I doing in my boxers and socks? Think, Jay. I was supposed to be on a plane headed for Switzerland with Bernard at my side. Instead, I'm half-naked at home, and Bernard's looking at me as if I just popped out of the womb. There's got to be a gap in my memory somewhere.

Oh shit, it all comes back to me. The men in black chasing me, the bald giant, the right-cross to the snout. Gradually, I begin to focus. Bernard is talking, but not to me. A chick comes out of my bathroom. Blonde, no more than five-four, cute, small boobs, pretty. Late twenties, tops. What's she doing here? She shakes her head, making her hair twirl. Her jeans and red blouse are a tight fit. I like her. I prick up my ears.

"Happy now, sir?"

Is it me, or is she taking the rise out of the old man?

"Thank you. Sleeping Beauty has finished his nap," snaps Bernard.

Hey! I've had some nicknames in my time, but none that have so offended my alpha male sensitivities. The chick looks at me like a dog eyeing a juicy steak. Get an eyeful, baby. Make the most of it.

"A hot little Beauty," she opines.

They'd better cut out the Beauty stuff right now. It's my cue. "Why am I in my bed? Why were two guys chasing me? How come you're here, Bernard? And who's Buffy?"

"Four questions on the bounce. I'm glad to see you're fully functioning again. Allow me to reply, one by one. You're in your bed because someone put you here after knocking you out cold. Your two attackers are dead. Their bodies have vanished into thin air somehow. I'm here because your Good Samaritan called me. He found my number in your cell phone. As for 'Buffy,' her name's Jackie, and she'll be your chaperone for the trip to Switzerland."

Bernard's talking faster than usual. Is he worried? If so, who for? Himself or me? "Your bag wasn't touched. Grab a shower and an aspirin and get to the airport with Jackie. I'm staying in New York to coordinate the whole show."

I get up. Holy shit, Jackie really is tiny. I thought the Secret Service was pickier about the people they let in. "Sorry, miss, but… Bernard, are you sure she's gonna be my guardian angel? The two goons and the Jolly Green Giant were in the superheavyweight category." I quickly fill him in on the chase and my rescue by the giant stranger.

"Give me more on the giant," he says.

"A white Michael Jordan, huge and incredibly agile for his size. I wasn't in the best position to give you his precise stats." Bernard nods but says nothing. The chick moistens her lips as she looks me up and down.

"Jackie will take good care of you. Don't be fooled by her size, or you'll be in for a surprise. Powwow over.

Get into that shower and get going. Your flight leaves JFK at 5:25. You arrive at 7:25 tomorrow morning, local time."

Seems like I never get to choose anymore. It's a pain in the ass. I grab a smoke from the pack on the nightstand and light it up. "What about Mom?" I pull hard on my cigarette.

"I'll tell you all about it in the car. Promise. Go!"

Twenty minutes later, I'm back in Bernard's car. My chaperones are up front, like Mommy and Daddy. I'm little Jimmy in the back. Cool. With a teddy bear and a coloring book, I'd be ready for summer camp.

As soon as Bernard pulls away from the curb, he keeps his word and spills the beans. They think Mom was poisoned at the hospital by a woman disguised as a nurse. The security camera tapes are being studied to identify the suspect. He'll know more when the results come through. To conclude, he recaps: Dad dies god knows how, Mom's murdered, and some creeps are after me. Bernard's conclusion is irrefutable.

The Corbin is an endangered species.

§ § §

At the wheel of his pickup, Eytan had been idling for a good ten minutes a hundred or so yards behind Bernard Dean's 7 Series.

111a: surveillance. 111b: protection.

Assassination, he knew. Abduction and exfiltration, he loved. Protection, this was his first time. Questions multiplied in his mind, but there were no answers. Over the last few weeks, he'd gathered scraps of information like pieces of a huge jigsaw that didn't want to fit together.

He was certain of one thing, at least. Jeremy was at the heart of this whole business. He was the bait for a big, very big, predator.

CHAPTER 13

Behind his small steel-rimmed spectacles, he watched the learned assembly of scientists, archeologists and historians squabbling. The central theme of the meeting was: *Was the Cloak of Odin, God of Gods of Asgard, in Finland or Norway?* The question was important enough for some of the contributors to be ready to come to blows over it. The situation didn't displease the *reichsführer-SS*. He found the posturing of these hopeless lice incredibly amusing. Since the order had been founded three years earlier, sterile debate and far-fetched projects had been the only items on the agenda. Nonetheless, the Study Society for Primordial Intellectual History represented a major step in furthering ethnic purification and would undoubtedly engender the Reich's complete racial superiority.

Unfortunately, from the inauguration to today's bickering, nothing good had come of it. Dangerous and costly missions had been carried out across the world. All had been unspeakable failures. Heinrich Himmler recalled his dream of finding the hammer of the Nordic god of thunder, Thor. What an idiot! And now, just to curry favor with the SS leader, a whole collection of knuckleheads was making the same mistake. Pathetic! The hopes of the Reich's *de facto* deputy leader now rested with the exploration of the Tibetan plateau led by Ernst Schäfer, a zoologist well traveled in Tibet who was devoted to Nazism and corresponded better with Heinrich's idea of a scientist: bold, calm and hard-working. With any luck, the expedition would find traces of the Aryan race and, hopefully, the mythical city of Shambhala and its myriad treasures.

The führer had been piling on the pressure for months. Heinrich was running out of dumb excuses to buy time. Fortunately, the *Anschluss*, planned for March, would give Adolf something to chew on. Not to mention the inevitable consequences of Germany's annexation of Austria. One way or another, the international community would react, and Hitler would stop obsessing about the Study Society's deliberations. These mind-numbing meetings full of maniacs would be no more than a bad memory.

Two archeologists grabbed each other's collars. Two historians struggled to separate them. Pathetic. Heinrich battled to stifle a huge yawn that could have disastrous consequences. Dampening all this enthusiasm would be counterproductive. Channeling it was vital. At this stage of extreme boredom, wiping his spectacles with a handkerchief was the only possible distraction. With his glasses in his hands, he couldn't see a thing. He hated his shortsightedness and, more generally, his fragile body so far removed from the Teutonic ideal he sought to propagate. On his orders, the SS recruited nobody under five feet, ten inches. He was two inches shy of that standard. Fate had dealt him a lousy hand, but his industrious and methodical mind compensated for that injustice.

His spectacles back in place, Heinrich scanned the hall. His Generals Hall filled him with pride. He wanted to make the castle, leased for a pittance, a center of excellence for SS officers. Renovations were under way, and soon every wing would be a hive of activity that would be decisive for the Order's future. The golden disk encrusted in a marble circle on the floor and the timeworn stone pillars conferred on the building the requisite mystical solemnity. Sunk into deep alcoves, the windows glowed in the moonlight. In three or four years, Wewelsburg would be ready. Heinrich would leave to the next generations an architectural masterpiece and wonder of organization. But for the moment, parasites sullied the place.

Heinrich was on the verge of exploding. He was thinking that only a couple of executions for sedition would appease him when he heard a cough. Turning his head to the right, poised to take the person to task, he saw Hermann Müller standing at attention, squeezed into a uniform too tight for a man of his obesity. His neck oozed over his collar. His ruddy cheeks seemed to indicate imminent heart failure. Quite simply, he looked like Göring. Müller was in charge of interdepartmental liaison in the castle. A position only he believed to be of crucial importance.

Next to the tub of lard, a young man shuffled from one foot to the other. Intimidated or desperate for the toilet, Heinrich couldn't decide. Then, snapping his heels and stretching out his arm, the baby elephant screeched *"Heil Hitler"* without interrupting the enthusiastic gibbering taking place five yards away.

"Heil Hitler," came the *reichsführer's* limp response.

"Herr Himmler, may I introduce you to a scientist worthy of the greatest interest?"

"That depends on your ability to distinguish the interesting from the superfluous."

"You won't be disappointed, Excellency. I assure you." Müller almost dared to look outraged.

Such boldness from a notorious yes-man piqued Heinrich's curiosity. A quick glance over Müller's shoulder confirmed that the debate had degenerated into a boxing match. "Fine, I'll listen. I hardly have anything better to do," Heinrich sighed. "But let's spice up the encounter, shall we? Hermann, you wager your life on the relevance of what this person has to say." The fat paper-pusher sputtered, miraculously avoiding a heart attack. *Shame*, thought the *reichsführer-SS*. *That would have saved a bullet.*

Heinrich examined the young man. The threat didn't seem to overawe him in the slightest. "Name and position." Revitalized by his bet, Heinrich's voice rang out.

"Bleiberg, Viktor, researcher in nuclear physics and chemistry. I study with Otto Hahn at Berlin University."

Wonderful, a student! "How old are you?" The affable tone barely concealed Heinrich's despair. "Twenty-one, sir," the boy replied nonchalantly.

Müller was sweating profusely.

"Sir," continued the young scholar.

"Your Excellency, if you don't mind." The icy smile promised imminent pain.

"Yes, sorry, Your Excellency. Don't allow my age to undermine the importance of what I have to say. I matriculated at the university at the age of fifteen. Professor Hahn considers me his best student. I have my own research lab, you know." Pride shone on his juvenile features.

Heinrich Himmler felt his interest perking up. Events in the rest of the room faded. Nothing existed except the scientist's voice. Instinctively, Himmler sensed that the young man possessed vital information. "What does he have you working on?"

"The consequences of brief exposure to radiation on the human body, Your Excellency."

"Continue." The SS's undisputed leader sat up.

"I have pursued Madame Curie's experiments with polonium and radium from the period 1909 to 1914."

"Spare me the lecture, thank you," Himmler sniped, waving his hand to dismiss any temptation the scientist might have had to continue in that vein.

"Yes, OK. We know the human body reacts negatively to radiation exposure. However, if we succeed in controlling cell necrosis, we can envisage important biological transformations."

"I read Marie Curie's reports, and I have followed Otto Hahn's work for some time. Your hypothesis is interesting but purely speculative. So far, there have been no conclusive results and no positive experiments in the area that interest me. Moreover, medical ethics are holding back research."

"With all due respect, Your Excellency, if we bypassed the ethical concerns of the stick-in-the-muds at the university, our chances of success would improve tremendously. Naturally, we'd have to close our eyes to—how can I put it—certain unedifying practices." A perverse grin accompanied his sly suggestion. The boy might be cracked. He was certainly no choirboy.

Himmler steepled his fingers in front of his mouth. "Let's put our cards on the table, shall we? My time is precious, and I am in no mood to waste it today. Professor Bleiberg, what do you expect from me?"

"I'm asking Your Excellency to appoint me head of a research unit on human mutation. In case you should approve my request, I've prepared a list of all that I require. Furthermore, I wish to work according to moral stipulations that I alone shall decide. In science, I believe necessity knows no law."

"I see. And what can I hope for in return?"

"An *Übermensch*, Your Excellency."

The *reichsführer* heaved a sigh. "You think your experiments will lead to a superman? As I said, young man, the scientific foundations are shaky."

"Not any more, Your Excellency. Not since last month." No smile had ever been smugger.

Himmler leaped up. "Are you telling me…"

"Yes, Your Excellency. I still need to improve my formula, but thanks to controlled exposure to radiation, with a chemical additive, I am able to improve, stably and permanently, the performances of the human body."

CHAPTER 14

That bitch killed Mom. Bernard showed me the screen captures from the hospital security tapes sent to his cell phone. He expects the autopsy results to confirm his hunch. While I'm on a plane headed to the Old World, a doctor's chopping up my mother and digging around in her organs. The urge to puke makes my gut spasm.

Strangely, my heart in my mouth, tears choking in my throat, I feel whole today. Despite the grief, guilt and the killers on my heels, I feel alive. I want to live. I need to unravel my father's secrets, slaughter the woman who killed my mother and unmask the shadowy figures behind all this. Oh yes, I nearly forgot. And smash my fist into the hairless giant's face.

"Very pleasant, business class." My neighbor stretches like a cat. She is dwarfed by the huge seat. Ouch, she's expecting a reply. I can see it in her eyes.

"I think three grand one way per person allows us to expect a little comfort."

She pouts. It suits her. "Money. That's all men ever think of, isn't it?"

I glance at her small but firm chest filling her shirt. "Not exactly. You'd be surprised by the number of young women who share that passion."

"Count me out."

Really? An exception. "OK. What does it for you? Sports cars, a beach home in Florida, ripped six-pack abs?"

"None of the above. I like guns. The moment the bullet shoots out, the slight recoil tingling in my wrist and up to my shoulder. Mmmm."

She's nuts! "Whatever floats your boat," I mumble, fiddling with the controls to recline my seat.

She lets out a melodious giggle. "I'm kidding. Bernard warned me you weren't a laugh a minute, but I didn't expect to travel with an undertaker." She glances up at me.

Sprawled across the arm of the seat, she looks like she's about to rip my shirt off. "Hey, you want a quick flashback on my life? Bernard did brief you, didn't he?"

"Sure. He is amazingly organized, and his records are second to none. You're right, your file beats all comers for twisted, unfunny shit. I can't decide what's saddest—your dad leaving home or the car accident that killed the little girl."

She's crossed the line. Screw my fantasies. Either I punch her, or I jump out of the plane to get away from her. Before I can react, she rubs salt into the wound. "Can't escape me, huh? That must be annoying. And it's tricky to get in a good shot in such a cramped space. I really feel sorry for you."

Can she read my mind? I lean closer. There's no point letting the entire business class hear. "Listen up, Buffy. We have another five hours on this plane. If you back off, you'll be doing us both a favor. Are you here to keep me safe or bust my balls?"

She wipes that shit-eating grin off her face. Leans closer, too. Her lips brush against my ear. Now I'm tingling. "There are two instances when a guardian angel is no use. When an assailant is prepared to die in order to take out the target. And when the target is just begging to die. Your file amply demonstrated your vulnerability to suicidal impulses. Bernard gave me a mission, and I intend to see it through. I can't do it without you on my side."

"How does that explain your half-assed wisecracks?"

"A suicide case doesn't bust a gasket when you grind his gears."

Busted! Pop psychology CIA-style. Signs of intelligent life detected. Looks like we have a match on our hands.

§ § §

Aboard the same plane, Eytan was cursing economy and its seats for dwarves and children. Fortunately, the airlines separated the wheat from the chaff and spared business class passengers the sight of the plebeians cramped in the back of the plane. Unfolding his knees when they arrived in Switzerland would demand a superhuman effort.

Meanwhile, he'd focus his anger on the brat poking his tongue out at him while playing on his video-game console.

DAY 3

CHAPTER 15

Securing an appointment had proved complicated. The prisoner's agenda was full to overflowing. To think he was serving a sentence for an attempted putsch in Bavaria. It was more like he was leading a rally in the middle of Munich. Too much!

Wide-eyed, Christian Delmar peered at the visitors standing in line. Everything seemed to indicate that his organization hadn't chosen to send him to see this man by accident. Delmar exchanged an incredulous smile with his Spanish acolyte, who had the unpronounceable Basque name Adamet Epartxegui. The two emissaries had met for the first time ten minutes ago and once their mission was accomplished would probably never see each other again. They shared complete mastery of the German language and veneration of a common ideal. Furthermore, both were in their early twenties and concealed their youth under hats and behind mustaches.

After they had waited patiently for an hour, a guard asked them to follow him. He was considerably taller than both visitors. Christian felt uncomfortable facing this mountain of muscle, made inoffensive only by the hooded eyelids signifying limited cerebral capacity. Adamet—Christian had given up trying to remember his last name—instinctively drew closer to his superior. The crowded jail, harsh lights and rancid odor of soup gave the emissaries nausea. A labyrinth of gray hallways and iron gates led them to the building's third west wing. With every step, the cold began to pinch a little more.

The guard stopped outside cell No. 7. To Christian's amazement, he knocked on the door. A long silence followed. Then a barked command came from inside the cell. The voice carried a natural authority that accentuated the surrealism of the scene. A man with incredibly bushy eyebrows and a square, thrusting jaw opened the door, standing ramrod straight before them.

"Hess!" That was a typically German way of introducing himself, with his last name and no preamble or beating around the bush.

"We have an appointment with Herr Hitler. We are Delmar and Adamet." The Basque didn't balk at the use of his first name. It seemed to Christian that remaining anonymous suited his colleague.

"Please come in, gentlemen. Adolf Hitler is expecting you." With a military gesture, Hess ushered the visitors into the cell. Christian was no longer surprised to discover that "cell" was hardly the right word. Against the left wall stood a large desk with two vases filled with flowers whose name escaped him. To the right, under the double window facing the door, was a perfectly made-up white iron bed. Either Hitler had fond memories of his military years, or the prison authorities provided him with a chambermaid. Delmar stifled his undiplomatic urge to laugh. On the table next to the bed, there was an Art Deco lamp, and a rug lay on the floor. The warmth of the room contrasted with the pervasive icy cold in the rest of the penitentiary and the whole of Bavaria, for that matter.

His head propped in his hand, an average-sized man leaned on the windowsill, observing the horizon through the gray bars. The sling supporting his left arm was a legacy of the authorities' brutality at the moment of his arrest. Logically, Hitler should have been a dead duck after his putsch failed. What was happening could only convince the prisoner that his future was bright.

Christian stared at the immobile figure. Hair shaved over his ears and nape and flopping over his forehead, neatly knotted tie and crisply ironed collar, uniform pants and black suspenders. Adolf the putschist looked like an accountant, insignificant and featureless even. The tuft of a mustache under his nose, protruding chin and a mouth like a scar across his face did nothing to contradict first impressions. But the gleam in his eyes revealed the extraordinary will of a man convinced of his destiny. Christian Delmar had studied history. What did all men of his type have in common? Madness as their only companion.

For one long minute, deafening silence occupied the room. Hitler seemed miles away, unaware of their presence or ignoring it as unimportant. While Herr Hess glared at the two visitors, who stared, in turn, at their feet, a voice that brooked no argument shattered the silence. "Your company asked me to grant an appointment to two emissaries. You're here. I'm listening, gentlemen."

No room for niceties. Christian spoke up. "Your entourage includes members of our organization. They have informed us of your ideas, your—how can I put it?—vision of the future."

"Get to the point. Other people are waiting." The accompanying dismissive gesture especially irritated Christian. The Frenchman cleared his throat and continued. "Yes, our superiors are willing to lend you the support you require to take power."

"You have my attention now." Hitler knew how to smile. The atmosphere warmed slightly.

"You will receive funding, the backing of the business sector and logistical and operational support for your party. If necessary, your opponents and rivals could be neutralized or even eliminated."

"I shall crush my enemies! The court could have sent me before a firing squad. Instead, it chose to salute my patriotism, my love for greater Germany. It's not the party that concerns me. I need an army, not sheep in wolf's clothing whose bombastic speeches disguise their absence of ambition. The German people deserve more than the wretched peace the Versailles Treaty forced upon us." Hitler punctuated his words with abrupt gestures, as if his forearms had a mind of their own. He jabbed his finger threateningly at his visitors. The dice had been rolled.

"Let's be clear. We won't raise a finger to help you if you refuse to respect the political rules in force in your country. You must follow a legal path to power in order to benefit from our assistance. We will have no problem finding another leader to achieve our aims. Herr Hitler, either you are with us, or you are against us. There is no middle ground." Christian anticipated another outburst of anger. The only response he received was a smile.

"Might your organization be as influential as Rudolf claims? I assumed you were madmen in the thrall of esotericism, but it seems to me now that you are looking for more than cheap thrills." He was turning on the charm. Unpredictable and unfathomable. A real threat.

"Our organization is light-years from the clubs for aristocrats titillated by Ouija boards. We have shared values, Herr Hitler. Our objective and yours are linked by the quest for the superiority of the Aryan race. Working together would advance both our causes."

Rudolf Hess and Adolf Hitler shared a knowing look that testified to a growing interest in Christian Delmar's arguments. "Let's suppose I accept your offer. What would you require in return?"

"Nothing you can't give us."

"I'll be the judge of that!" Another unexpected outburst. The emissaries remained unperturbed.

"As I said, nothing you can't give us. You will take power by legal means, and you will be free to do what you want with it. You will apply the twenty-five-point program you had the NSDAP adopt in 1920. The future of the Jews is little concern to us. Kill them, imprison them, whatever you want. However, the anticapitalist measures must be revoked or disavowed."

"The economy is irrelevant. The State must control everything."

"A serious mistake, sir. You will need the support of industry, the banks and businessmen in order to develop your greater Germany. This aspect of our agreement is nonnegotiable."

Hess was about to intervene but remained silent. Hitler rubbed his chin and stared at the floor. "I'll think about it. What else?"

"You will institute scientific research programs in the military, industrial and, very importantly, medical fields. You will fund these programs with our support in both raw materials and hard cash. In return, we will be informed of every plan, formula and invention. We won't compromise on that either."

"On this point, our intentions converge. However, I fail to grasp the connection between your offer and your interest in the Germanic race."

"Our organization pursues the same objective as you, Herr Hitler."

"A new Germany?"

"No, Herr Hitler. A new world."

CHAPTER 16

The arrival at Zurich was torture. After fighting the urge to beat the crap out of his idiot neighbor throughout the flight—and the brat's incredibly lax mother at the same time—Eytan had to let everybody get off the plane before him to avoid being spotted by Jeremy Corbin. His nerves were frazzled, his knees had seized up, and he was ten minutes behind the stock trader. To add to his frustration, he had left all his weapons in NYC and wouldn't be resupplied until he arrived at the hotel his people had booked for him.

Fortunately, his surveillance job was facilitated considerably by the sheer predictability of an American agent. The young woman accompanying Jeremy would follow her CIA training to the letter. As a result, she would refuse to take a cab, renting a vehicle and driving it herself. That way, if they were followed, she would be in control of the situation. And she could carry weapons in the trunk. All Eytan had to do was head for the car-rental counter. A sardonic smile on his face, his habitual military bag over his shoulder, Eytan walked through the airport, wondering why he was whistling "The Colonel Bogey March." As he approached the car-rental counters, he slowed and slipped behind a pillar. The international terminal would soon be swamped with passengers, but for now only a few shambling groups were visible, making his surveillance task all the easier.

The two blonds were filling in forms at the desk. Hanging around to watch was pointless. Eytan left the building. The air was warm. The temperature would reach the seventies in the afternoon. Summer wasn't Eytan's favorite season. His massive build was better suited to cooler climates. He climbed into a cab, quickly explained, in perfect German, that his wife would soon appear with her handsome lover and handed the cabbie a bundle of euros. The driver's sympathetic look received a blank response.

While keeping an eye on the parking garage exit, Eytan considered the possibilities. The Swiss were known for their watches, cheese and, above all, their banks. Could Jeremy and his chaperone be here to recover the documents the Metsada had been chasing after for weeks?

A gray Lexus coupe stopped at the parking garage barrier. The tinted windows made identifying the occupants impossible. Eytan hesitated. He needed to be absolutely certain. The passenger window was lowered. A barely smoked cigarette flew out and bounced on the asphalt. The window closed immediately but not before Eytan had glimpsed Jeremy's hair. The Israeli agent relaxed, tapped the cabbie on the shoulder, and off they went.

§ § §

"Yada yada yada," grumbled Jeremy.

"You're not just a pig; you're a puerile one." Jackie's tone was serious. This time, she wasn't playing mind games.

"Look who's talking. After half a day on a plane, I think I'm allowed to enjoy a smoke. Jesus wept!"

"You can wait till we arrive. All I can say is, the car's no-smoking. End of story." With a resigned sigh and a final drag, Jeremy lowered the window and flicked the cigarette away. "Now what?"

"We swing by the hotel, pick up the gear left by... No, that's none of your business. Caffeine refill and a visit to the bank. If all goes as planned, we'll be on the flight home at one this afternoon."

"Cool. There's no point hanging around. I want to be back for Mom's funeral."

Jeremy stiffened, fighting a wave of grief.

"I understand. But..." Jackie hesitated, as if sincerely regretting what she was about to say. "There's next to no chance Bernard will allow you to attend. You'd be playing into the hands of the people gunning for your family. Bernard wants to keep the lid on my assignment with you, so he won't agree to a major protection operation or even lay a trap for your enemies."

"I can't let her go without saying good-bye, Jackie. No way. She raised me on her own, and I was never in the running for Son of the Year. I owe it to her."

Jackie remained silent. Jeremy interpreted it as a mark of compassion—an unexpected one, at that. When she spoke, her tone had changed. "We're being followed."

"What?"

"A black Mercedes on our tail. I've been changing lanes and ignoring the GPS for the last few miles, just driving at random. We're not dealing with a genius, but he can drive."

"Do you have a plan?" Jeremy realized just how small she looked behind the huge wheel.

"Unarmed, it's better to avoid contact. Dammit, we're passing up a great opportunity to snare them and find out more."

"Them? You don't think it's my giant?"

"From what you said and Bernard's reaction, I don't see that guy letting himself be spotted so easily."

"What do we do?"

"Let them follow us. Forewarned is forearmed. We're ahead of the game."

§ § §

A Peugeot taxi tailing a Lexus that was being followed by a Mercedes. The situation verged on the ridiculous. Eytan smiled. They were doing everything to make life easy for him. Blondie would be watching the Merc, not him. The pursuers, who were anything but smart apparently, wouldn't pay any attention to him either.

So far, so good. A little inner voice whispered to Eytan, *For how long?*

CHAPTER 17

They're still on our ass. Jackie says there's no point trying to lose them. I feel like a worm on a hook. Not a fate I envy. Note to self: Cool car, this Lexus. If I make it out of this and can sit behind a wheel again, I'll buy one to replace my DB9.

We reach the hotel with them on our tail. Thank God, it's an underground parking garage. They don't push their luck by following us in. Blondie's right. They're waiting for us to recover whatever's in the safe-deposit box before hitting us like a swarm of locusts on a field of wheat. If I had to choose, I'd take the locusts. But you don't always get what you want.

I've decided to let events take their course. If I'm gonna die, I'm gonna die. I can't see my pocket-size bodyguard stopping a colossus riddling me with bullets. We'll see. In any case, she's got the discreet surveillance of her surroundings down pat. Good job.

The hotel's pure luxury. I don't know about the city. I only saw it reflected in a rearview mirror. At least I've got a Swiss stamp in my passport now. I can start a collection. The elevator takes us straight to the lobby. Big, clean and shiny. Hip mirrors on the walls. I was hoping for a Swiss chalet, and I wind up in a cookie-cutter boutique. We could be anywhere in the world. It's almost sad. The standard desk and receptionist seen a thousand times before. Jackie registers us as Mr. and Mrs. Ingalls. The guy doesn't notice my look of surprise. Charles and Caroline Ingalls—alcoholic trader and CIA killer. Shit's going down in *The Little House on the Prairie*. I lean back six degrees to scope her butt. Nice. A married man now, but don't expect me to be sawing wood just yet. Best of all, the CIA's picking up the tab. If killers weren't chasing me, my parents hadn't just died, and I didn't feel like a rat in a maze, I'd almost think I was on vacation.

A bellhop appears with a black case. Jackie smiles. Tooled up. The bellhop accompanies us to our room. On the way to the elevators, I check out the wildlife in the lobby. Actually, I stare at it. Which of these "guests" is going to stab me in the back? Is the bitch that killed my mother here? And the little fat guy with greasy hair in the badly cut suit, why's he staring at me like that? I'm sweating. My right hand starts to shake. They could use some AC in here. The heat's unbearable. The way my guts are torturing me, the in-flight meal must have been past its sell-by date.

Jesus, quit staring, you asshole! He's coming over, reaching into his jacket. He's a hit man! Jackie's up ahead. I yell, but she doesn't look around. The bellhop's feeling up her ass. She's stripping in public. A freak, I knew it. You'll have Jay jumping your bones, beauty! But right now, I charge the dwarf before he smokes me. Tackle him to the floor. He lashes out with his tentacles. Shit, is his skin blue? The world's spinning around me. Suddenly, once again, the lights go out.

§ § §

"Hey!" A sudden burning sensation wakes me.

"There you go, Jeremy. You'll feel better in a few minutes." Jackie's leaning over me. A strange newly kind tone in her voice. She's holding an empty syringe.

"Better? What happened to me? I was in the lobby and then... I don't know, everything just went weird."

"Cold turkey. With the stress and jet lag you got a fit of something like delirium tremens. I gave you a shot of a derivative of benzodiazepine. You need to drink some sugar water and get some glucose into your system. From now until we get back to New York, you'll have to carry a bottle of water with you at all times."

She presses a cotton ball to my forearm. The fleeting skin contact makes my whole body tingle. Unless it's the stuff she just injected into me. "You always walk around with that on you?"

"Hardly. I thought it might come in handy. Bernard warned me about your alcohol issues. I thought I'd better have something with me just in case. Anticipation's an important part of my profession."

"You're doing a fine job."

"I wish I could return the compliment. You attacked a hotel guest. Keeping him quiet will cost the American taxpayer. Incidentally, you also called me a horny bitch and announced your plans for me. Very classy."

Ouch. I grab the pillow, wedge it against the headboard and haul myself into a sitting position. The gyroscope's still off-center, and the room pitches like a sailboat in a storm.

"No way are you getting out of that bed. The jab is palliative not curative."

I massage my temples and close my eyes, hoping the first signs of a headache will go away. When I open them, Jackie's in the bathroom doorway, a damp towel in her hand and an affectionate smile on her lips.

"Does this benzo shit have any known side effects?" Silently, she comes over and presses the towel to my forehead. Cool water trickles over my cheekbones, follows the contours of my jaw and drips onto my chest.

"Sure. Sleepiness, loss of balance, dependence if you keep on using it. But you'll be OK with the dose I gave you. You've just succeeded in making my job a bit more difficult." I grasp her wrist with one hesitant hand and look her in the eyes. Adopting a serious expression isn't hard for me right now.

"I'm sorry, Jackie. For the insults and anything else I said." She doesn't reply, except with a look every bit as intense and sincere as mine. The skin contact flusters her as much as me. Usually I'd shamelessly take advantage, but not with her.

Snapping out of it, my chaperone stands up. "Don't worry. The sexual fantasies are caused by the delirium. I'm not mad at you. We'll stay here this morning to let you recover and head over to the bank after lunch. And along with drinking all that water, you'll have to stay away from the booze. The drug and alcohol don't mix."

Barely twenty minutes later, I'm on my feet again, not without a slight but mercifully brief loss of balance. I grab a smoke at the window, watching the avenue down below. Jackie locked herself in the bathroom shortly after shooting that shit into me. I sound harsh, I know. Must be the jet lag.

The bathroom door opens, and my water nymph emerges reinvigorated, with damp hair and wearing anthracite-colored jeans and a pale blue shirt. White sneakers with pink stripes emphasize how small her feet are. She wears a few discreet touches of makeup and even a little gloss on her delicate lips. I should feel flattered and smile—it's always a good sign when a woman dolls herself up—but my mind's full of morose thoughts. This moment of solitude, a rare luxury since yesterday, has allowed me to get things straight in my head. I was wrong about everything the whole time. My father, my mother, Bernard. The fatal accident I caused is the action that best reflects my true self. That's nothing to smile about.

"Stop beating yourself up. You really think that'll bring her back?"

She's an expert at reading my mind and catching me off guard. I fiddle with my cigarette to hide my melancholy ruminations.

"At the risk of coming across as a total douchebag—or more of one than I appear to be already—I have to confess the aim isn't to bring her back. Unfortunately, that's beyond my, or anyone else's, power. Until that crappy night, I'd been wasted a couple of times in my whole life. Sober, there would have been no accident. Drunk, my reaction time was too slow. That's what eats me up. Guys get wasted every weekend with no consequences except the gradual destruction of their livers. Me, it took one drunken party and a momentary distraction to kill a child. I have to live with that on my conscience. I have no choice. I don't drink as a cop-out, but as appropriate punishment. But have no fear, I don't drive anymore."

My smile doesn't seem to convince her or dampen her curiosity. Understandable. I don't convince myself. She wants to know more. "How did you beat the rap? Shouldn't you be in jail?"

I need nicotine. I take a big drag on my smoke. "Bernard offered the parents a one-off lump sum. A very big sum. A PI the firm hired found out the mother was an undocumented immigrant. Cash plus silence equals Jeremy dodges jail time. And it makes me sick."

As disgust deforms my features, I try to get a grip. Jackie sees the evil gnawing away at me. Her voice softens. "You never talk about it, do you?"

She's sharp as a tack. It might as well come out. "No. Never seriously. You know, Jackie, hating yourself doesn't make life easy. And admitting it doesn't solve anything." She comes over, grins, nudges me aside and peers out the window with me. She's happy pressing up against me. The feeling of her thigh against mine is up there in the Highlights of My Existence.

"You're wrong about two things."

"Oh, yeah? Which ones, Miss Freud?"

She slicks back her damp hair, then shakes her head left and right. "Hurting people comes easy for some heavy drinkers. My father proved that time and again." Buffy isn't looking at me. Her gaze wanders over the buildings opposite us. I expect the worst. "He started hitting me in my high school freshman year. Occasional beatings, followed by endless apologies and sobbing. There was nothing he had to take out on anybody. He was a doctor in deepest, darkest Arkansas, a respected, well-liked figure, a regular churchgoer. He had money, a wife who loved him and a hardworking daughter. But he drank for no apparent reason. The asshole blamed it on me. He said I was too pretty, a prick tease. Believe me, I was so shy it was almost impossible for a boy to talk to me."

I let out a long whistle. "I get the picture."

She arches an eyebrow and looks at me with doe eyes. "To some extent, what happened shaped the rest of my life. To cover up the bruises, I found something to justify them. I started attending the tae kwon do class that some madman had opened in that nowhere town. I got into it, and the instructor said I had talent. One day, I came home and saw that my father was treating my mother the same as me. He didn't see the first blow coming. Nor any of the blows that followed. I kicked his ass all over the house. I stopped just before I killed him. I didn't hate him enough to rot in jail for life on a murder rap. He dragged himself along the floor, beat up and bleeding, begging me, telling me my mother understood him. How long had she been taking the slaps and lashes of his belt? I didn't give him time to justify himself. I didn't see any point listening to his pathetic excuses. I grabbed some stuff and walked out. I joined the army, then the Secret Service before Bernard recruited me. He got me a transfer to the CIA's Special Operations Unit after he saw my file at a disciplinary hearing for insubordination. I have problems with authority. Ever since, every opponent has my father's face. I made anger my greatest motivation."

"I conclude it's better not to pick a fight with you."

"It's not necessarily a good idea. Why the long face? My story isn't so dramatic."

Oh yeah? I have a long face? I'd better watch myself, but the thought of a guy hitting this girl revolts me. Hugging her seems the only thing to do. Anyway, let's change the subject. "And the other point?"

"When you behave like a human being, you're not at all objectionable. Now get dressed. I ordered room service. We'll leave for the bank as soon as we've eaten."

I like being with this woman. I feel good at her side. With her, I'm not anxious or on edge. She feels something for me, and that makes me happy. At least one piece of good news this week.

§ § §

Eytan pushed the right sleeve of his camouflage jacket up to the elbow. He heaved a sigh and let it fall back down to his wrist. The marks on his skin had always depressed him. Surgery could easily get rid of the ugly blemishes. But would he still be himself? He'd asked himself the same question dozens, even hundreds of times. It would haunt him as long he lived. That's why he hated inaction. With idleness, reminiscences wormed their way into his mind, slipping through the crack of boredom. And for the last two hours, Eytan had been bored stiff.

As usual, he'd picked up his gear as soon as he arrived at the hotel—the same one as the odd couple he was tailing. After loading up with guns and clips, he took a quick shower and shaved his head, chin and eyebrows. A chat with the receptionist revealed the lovebirds' room number and the strange fit Mr. Ingalls had thrown in the lobby, causing panic among the guests.

He couldn't say why, but Eytan was starting to feel a kind of affection for his "client." This walking-disaster case amused him. It was a change from the usual bastards he had to deal with—double agents, terrorists, shady diplomats.

The black Mercedes was still parked on the avenue outside the five-star hotel, with a perfect view of the parking garage exit. In theory, the tinted windows guaranteed its occupants' anonymity. In theory. Two hours' waiting didn't even touch the surface of Eytan's bottomless well of patience, but he had a furious urge to have some fun. He strode over to the Mercedes and knocked on the driver's window. A good twenty seconds later, it opened a fraction, barely an inch. Not enough to see inside.

"What do you want?" asked a baritone voice, speaking German in a dialect specific to the Zurich area. Luckily, Eytan knew some of its subtleties.

"Sorry to bother you. I'm looking for Grossmünster Cathedral. Which way is it?"

Another few seconds ticked by. "No idea. Ask in the hotel. Have a good day." Polite but brisk. The window closed to end the conversation. As he straightened up, Eytan's wallet dropped onto the road and skidded under the car. He cursed and hunkered down to pick it up.

With Eytan on his knees and stretched under the vehicle, the car's occupants could see only his broad back. Having retrieved his wallet, Eytan Morg stood up and gave a friendly wave in the direction of the taciturn driver.

Crossing back to the hotel, the agent grinned to himself. "Don't screw with me."

CHAPTER 18

The punch hit fresh air. The little blonde spun away from right hooks and uppercuts with astonishing ease. The guy's technique wasn't too shabby, but she was simply too fast for him. Overbalancing slightly, he pivoted and aimed another kick at the young woman. She blocked and immediately riposted with two straight lefts to her opponent's face.

Crouching behind one of the many trashcans on the dark street, Eytan enjoyed watching Blondie's athleticism, complete mastery of combat techniques and marvelous speed and coordination. Of course, she was in her current situation because of a glaring error that should have been fatal. Letting her pursuers catch up with her in this alleyway would get her bawled out by the worst instructor in the most pathetic intelligence service in the world. Luckily, rather than blowing her away, the two goons appeared to be under orders to capture her and get information out of her. Easier said than done.

The two guys were the slippery type. Lithe and sinewy, they were overconfident as they closed in on their prey. Before he could finish his sentence—inaudible from Eytan's vantage point—the first attacker was sucking up a headshot that sent him flying into the garbage bags, his nose a bloody mess. The second guy didn't make the same mistake, attacking cagily, his guard high.

As the ballet went on, Blondie continued to find openings, but her punches began to lack penetration. She wasn't dealing with a beginner. Toe to toe, the fight swung in the guy's favor. Eytan wondered why she didn't draw the pistol he glimpsed now and then under her jacket. Both of them were taking unnecessary risks in the hope of obtaining vital information. No prisoners was the only rule. A true professional wounds, interrogates, kills. By flouting the basics of the job, apprentice agents come to a sticky and early end. How many had he seen trip up by underestimating the realities of life in the field?

The guy with the smashed snout was coming around. And it looked like he'd learned his lesson. Sprawled in the garbage behind Blondie, he drew his gun. Eytan immediately leaped out of his hiding place, unsheathed two knives from his waistband and sprinted hard. Attacking from his position, with two leaping, spinning, spiraling warriors duking it out, was taking a risk even for a fighter of his caliber. To hell with discretion. Leaving a young lady to die here wouldn't further his investigation and would bring dishonor on him.

He covered the twenty yards in a flash. The first blade buried itself in the neck of the guy fighting Jackie, who stared in dismay as he keeled over, spurting blood. The second landed between the eyes of the first attacker, who slumped back into the garbage with no hope of a second resurrection.

Eytan stood facing Jackie, who looked like she didn't know whether to be grateful or afraid. "Agent Jacqueline Walls, you should be ashamed of yourself."

"You know me? Who are you?" she gasped, out of breath.

"A friend. For now. You messed up by letting Jeremy go into the bank alone. I don't know who these guys are, but they're not amateurs. Did you seriously think they wouldn't spot you? You hoped to catch them out by keeping an eye on Corbin from a distance?"

Jackie shrugged sheepishly. "Yeah, I guess."

"Incompetence and stupidity! You should have anticipated that a second surveillance team had been assigned to the job."

Before she could protest, Eytan went on, "You still have a lot to learn in the art of staying discreet. Now run along, and stick close to your client. I'll take care of the stiffs."

"You're with the Agency?"

"Not really."

Without batting an eye, Jackie drew and leveled her gun at Eytan's face. "Tell me who you are. Fast! I'm in no mood for bullshit games."

Eytan towered over her and stared into her eyes. "Child..."

In a flash, he grabbed the gun and twisted it back on its owner. It was so fast and controlled, Jackie couldn't resist.

"Strike fast." Another sudden movement knocked the young woman backward. At the same time, a slap sent the gun flying out of her hand. By the time Jackie's butt hit the deck, Eytan had caught the weapon and was pointing it at her.

"Kill without blinking." Eytan tossed the automatic into the trash. "Those are the basics of our trade. Do your job, and stay alert. I won't be able to get you out of every hole you dig. The stiffs are all yours now. My regards to Dean."

He turned and strode back to the street. Glancing over his shoulder, he saw Jackie picking herself up, already dialing a number, surprised to be breathing, most likely.

§ § §

The bank vault looks like Fort Knox. Armed guards at every steel door. Basically, the architect designed a marble-lined bunker. The Swiss are hospitable but a touch too obsequious. Wealth has that effect. I didn't catch his name, but it doesn't matter. Klavich, Kravich, something with a Slav ring to it. A tight ass. His pigeon-toed, knock-kneed shuffle proved it with every step. Like a master of ceremonies at the court of Louis XIV.

Along the way, I give a little wave to all the security cameras. It's dumb, but it cracks me up. I feel kind of buzzed—a side-effect of the gunk in Jackie's injection, maybe. In fact, I'm floating on air. Back to reality. One huge door, two guards and three cameras later, we enter the small box vault, as my escort calls it. Good news. I won't have to drag a huge parcel around with me. He steps aside and ushers me in. Hundreds of little doors line the walls. Boris—I've decided the name suits him—opens one up and removes a brown rectangular box about a foot long. He exits after pointing out the button I need to press when I'm done. I wonder if the john works the same way.

I remove the lid of what could be a regular shoebox. Inside, I find a gray file closed with a red tab, a road map folded in four and something the size of a pack of cigarettes wrapped in brown paper. I stuff everything into my backpack. I'll examine it later with Jackie.

I hit the button. Let's get outta here. Am I going to take a bullet in the head as soon as I set foot on the street?

CHAPTER 19

BERGHOF, THE OBSERSALZBERG, BAVARIAN ALPS, JANUARY, 1943.

"My faithful Heinrich, I am relieved that you survived this odious attack."

"Thank you, *mein Führer.*"

"Please, take a seat."

Himmler settled into one of the eight armchairs surrounding the small round table, on which cups of coffee had been served to Europe's two most powerful men. And yet the scene was grotesque. The Great Hall could hold a hundred people easily. Heinrich felt like a lead figurine lost in an oversized dollhouse. He hated the place. Of all the Nazi dignitaries, only he had refused to take a house nearby. All the usual bootlickers had rushed to buy homes to stay in the führer's good books: that morphine-addicted pig Göring; the competent and therefore dangerous Goebbels; the uptight military man Jodl; and many others who jostled for Hitler's mercurial affections.

How the hell could they put up with these pitifully overwrought decorations?

The Gobelins tapestries depicted crude hunting scenes. The green chairs clashed with the red carpet. The beamed ceiling seemed in danger of collapsing on the room's occupants at any moment. Heinrich already missed the martial atmosphere of his head-quarters in Westphalia. There, at least, he was the absolute sovereign who bowed before no man. The news he brought would make his conversation with Hitler tricky. For now, Heinrich's position was guaranteed by the boundless devotion of his troops and the rapid progress being made in his extermination program.

"How many men did you lose?"

"The losses aren't too heavy. Four members of my personal bodyguard and two soldiers from the camp."

"It's the work of the communists!" Stamping his foot, Hitler shouted at the top of his voice, "We must crush them too. Eliminate them with no mercy, one by one until there are no more!"

"*Mein Führer*, the communists had nothing to do with this. Goebbels gave you a version of the facts intended to bolster the army and our people in the march toward Moscow. Blaming the Bolsheviks serves our cause. I came to set out to you the true circumstances of the explosion."

Hitler froze. He swept the hair from his forehead, a sure sign of annoyance.

"What are you saying? Why wasn't I informed? How can one be expected to rule a nation with false information?" Predictably, Hitler took on his world-weary air and flopped into the chair opposite Heinrich. He had been developing more and more of these spoiled-child affectations.

"That is why I am here today, *mein Führer*. We are currently hunting down seditious agents within the *Abwehr* itself. Given the sensitive nature of the information, bringing it in person seemed more judicious than sending a telegram."

"Traitors in the ranks of the *Abwehr*. Nothing surprises me anymore. They've been sabotaging my work from the very beginning. You will unmask those responsible, won't you, Heinrich?" It wasn't a question but an order.

"I hope to expose Wilhelm Canaris shortly. We must be sure to net the whole ring before we act. Rest assured, the matter will be settled within the next few days."

"Good, good. So, tell me what really happened in Poland." Until now, the conversation had gone as expected. But storm clouds were gathering.

"Five years ago, I met a young scientist named Bleiberg who was working on the effects of radiation and chemicals on the human body. His research was worth taking further, so the SS invested colossal sums in the construction of a secret laboratory in the basement of Wewelsburg Castle. In the next two years, the research team made spectacular progress. Very soon, tests on prisoners became necessary. I therefore ordered that the experimentation center be moved to the camp hospital at Stutthof, near Danzig."

"Excellent. Communist and Israelite scum deserve no leniency. By the way, your scientist's name, Bleiberg, doesn't that sound Jewish?"

"I ordered an inquiry, which proved him to be a good German, *mein Führer*." Heinrich preferred a lie to a sterile debate. Yes, Bleiberg was Jewish. The SS would take care of him once his research was completed.

"Good, good. What happened then?"

"The tests on humans were unpredictable and..." Hitler gestured with his left hand to interrupt his subordinate. Heinrich thought he saw the hand shake.

"What tests are you talking about? What was the aim of all this mysterious research?"

"Professor Bleiberg claimed to be capable of modifying the human body to recreate the pure Aryan race as described in ancient writings."

"The Hyperboreans? How ironic! We have sent expeditions to the Orient looking for Shambhala, to the North and where else besides, hunting for the roots of the Germanic race, and you're telling me that science has solved the question? Why didn't you tell me about this earlier?"

"I wanted to be certain, *mein Führer*. Besides, with the French campaign and the planning and, er, difficulties of Operation Barbarossa, I didn't wish to add to the burden on your shoulders."

"As considerate as ever, Heinrich. I appreciate it."

Heinrich replied with the sympathetic smile that served him so well in all circumstances. Behind his little round glasses, it was impossible to guess what ideas were germinating and what ambitions he nurtured. God, he loved that!

"I have a substantial workload, also. There's no lack of conspiracies, and the organization of the Final Solution requires complete concentration to ensure no crucial logistical details are overlooked. The team at Degesch has worked hard to deliver the Zyklon B ahead of schedule. As a result, however, there was a delay while the gas chambers were being built. We barely avoided a situation that would have been detrimental to our objectives. In sum, we were both too busy to waste time with conjecture. I wanted to bring you a feasible project or abandon the whole operation and move onto something else."

"I see. Please, go on."

"For two years, none of the test subjects survived the mutation process. Some died from the exposure to radiation. Others were unable to withstand the injections following exposure. The medics gradually stabilized each step, but the subjects developed rampant cancer. Then, at the end of last year, Professor Bleiberg requested that I visit Stutthof because he had important news for me. He knows me well and is aware that if someone whistles, I rarely come running."

"Except when your master whistles." A subtle but significant reminder. Heinrich smiled once more.

"Indeed, *mein Führer*. So, I was convinced that a welcome surprise awaited me in Poland."

"Let's go straight to the conclusion, shall we? Jodl's waiting his turn for a briefing on the Russian Front."

Jodl? Let him wait. "Very well. One of the subjects had survived the radiation, tolerated the injections and had not been laid low by a tumor. Bleiberg mentioned a high long-term cancer risk but thought he could develop a serum to stop the cell necrosis. Subject 302 was brought in. A pure marvel, *mein Führer*. The professor had turned a spindly Jew with stereotypical racial characteristics into a sturdy blond child. Even his nose was no longer hooked."

"Are you sure the operation was genuine? I assume it could have been easy to introduce a decoy. We both know that scientists are adept at such trickery."

"That's why I insisted on the whole process being filmed and photographed. There is no room for doubt. Subject 302 is the first functional prototype of the *Übermensch*."

"Why isn't he here with you?"

Heinrich took a deep breath to gather his nerve. "The child came to me quite docilely and gave a perfect salute. Most likely to allay my suspicions. I approached and ruffled his hair. Suddenly, he seized my service weapon, and before we could stop him, he shot holes in the vats of chemicals in the laboratory. Explosions gutted the building. In the confusion, he escaped. I was lucky to get out alive. Bleiberg and his team scrambled to save their archives. Their corpses must be frozen in the ruins."

Adolf Hitler wearily rubbed his eyes. "You didn't capture the subject?"

"No, *mein Führer*. Two of my elite units are still scouring the area. He must have died or gotten help. We will leave no stone unturned."

"You almost had good news for me. I'm grateful for your honesty, Heinrich. Keep me informed of developments. Before I let you go, give me something to celebrate."

"Treblinka and Sobibor have achieved cruising speed. Auschwitz-Birkenau is functioning at full capacity. Zyklon B is proving a highly efficient alternative to carbon monoxide. I estimate that sixty percent of European Jews will be eliminated within two years. We could go even faster, but I wish to keep the healthy ones available as a labor force for the war effort."

"Good. Excellent. Leave me now, Heinrich. Tell my secretary to show Jodl in. We have a counteroffensive to prepare on the Eastern Front."

Heinrich Himmler rose in silence. After an impeccable salute, which elicited a distracted response and no eye contact, he strode away, down twin flights of steps and approached the heavy wooden door. Hitler's voice stopped him in his tracks. "Heinrich! Just out of curiosity, what is this *Übermensch* operation's code name?"

"The Bleiberg Project, *mein Führer*."

CHAPTER 20

Eytan took up position at a table against the window of the bar across the street from the bank. Traffic was dense, but his line of sight was relatively unimpeded. Anyway, it wasn't as if he would need a clear shot. The next five minutes would hold no surprises for him.

In the last fifteen minutes, he had met Bart, the waiter, and Léon, a recently widowed retired postal-service manager who spent his afternoons in the bar. They were sipping their coffee and about to play a game of dice when Eytan saw Jeremy come out of the bank, looking anxiously for Jackie's Lexus. The perfect target.

Léon's expertise at the game of Four Twenty-one saw him to victory in the first round. He was warming the dice in his cupped hands to start the second game when, outside, Jacqueline pulled over, and Corbin hopped in. Twenty yards behind, the black Mercedes was on their tail. It would intercept the Lexus at the first opportunity. Eytan was sure of it. Two bullets to each head, the documents stolen, case closed.

Triple one. Léon picked up where he had left off. Eytan took a black box the size of a lighter out of his pocket. The fingers of his right hand fiddled with it while the dice rolled out of the palm of his left hand onto the green baize tray between the two players. His thumb tightened on the box. A deafening explosion echoed around the street, followed by screeching brakes and honking horns. The bar's patrons, including Léon, rushed out and gawked at the black sedan in flames. Debris hovered in the air before falling like pathetic metal leaves onto the road.

Triple six.

I warned you guys not to screw with me.

§ § §

In the movies, a car going up in a ball of fire looks cool. In real life, too. Except for the occupants of the bomb on wheels, of course. I didn't jump when the explosion happened. I have enough sedative in my veins not to show a flicker of emotion for another few hours. Jackie, on the other hand, nearly jumped out of her seat. She seems totally on edge. When I got into the rental, she was sweating and looking ragged. Jeez, with her hair all mussed up she's even cuter. Buffy rammed her cell phone under my nose. "That your Jolly Green Giant?"

The photo's blurred. Surely the CIA can afford more sophisticated equipment for its agents. They've got it tough. Now let's take a closer look: broad back, camouflage jacket, lumberjack boots, combat pants. "No fashion sense, bald as a coot, six-six and dubious sense of humor? Yes, little lady, that's him. But how…"

"He saved my life in an alleyway next to the bank. I wanted to create a diversion and take down two guys following us. Instead, I screwed up. He shivved both guys and inflicted the humiliation of a lifetime on me. I sent the picture to Bernard for identification."

"Don't complain. At least, you didn't wind up on your ass and out cold."

She tucks away the cell. Purses her lips slightly. I'm beginning to read you now, baby. "You did wind up on your ass?"

"Zip it!" I zip it. But I laugh my ass off. Not Jackie.

"We head to the hotel, check out what was in the safe-deposit box, debrief with Bernard, and that's where you get off the joyride."

"That's not your decision to make. Don't pull any national security or classified information bullshit on me. I smell a rat. An official mission would get me what, five, ten bodyguards? Bernard's flying solo. Why? No idea. You either, I guess. So Baldy made a fool of you? I'd appreciate it if you didn't take it out on me."

Jackie is about to reply when her phone rings. *Mission Impossible* ringtone. I laugh again. "OK, give me a break."

"Jackie?"

"Yes, sir. Sorry, I was chatting with Jeremy."

No, Jeremy just busted your ass. Get it right.

"I got the picture you took. Where and when?"

"Zurich, sir. Roughly fifteen minutes ago. Have you been able to identify him?" Long silence.

"Yes. How did you spot him?" It's Jackie's turn to fall silent. This one's going to overtime.

"I didn't spot him. He came to my assistance. Who is this guy, sir? He seems very well informed about the Agency and remarkably efficient." Playful self-confident Jackie was gone. Meet serious, anxious Jackie.

"He goes by the name Eytan Morg. Christ, that's why his voice seemed so familiar on the phone. If he hasn't killed you already, he must be there as a friend. Thank your lucky stars for that."

"This Morg guy asked me to send his regards. Do you know him personally, sir? Who does he work for?"

"Yeah, I know him. We worked together once. Back in the day he was a Mossad agent. Now? I'll have to get back to you on that. Do you have the documents? Have you taken a look?"

"The contents of the box are in our possession. We'll proceed with the examination as soon as we regroup at the hotel." Oh, the rhetorical delights of a military training.

"I want you to report back in the hour. Then jump on the first flight home."

"Yes, sir. I didn't find anything on the two individuals who tried to eliminate me. Another unit was following us, but their car blew up in traffic. With all due respect, sir, what the hell is going on?"

"You tell me, Jackie. You have one hour."

CHAPTER 21

YAD VASHEM MEMORIAL, JERUSALEM, SIX MONTHS EARLIER.

The greenery reached up to embrace the clear blue cloudless sky. The contrast was more striking than ever. The wood and steel cattle car on a stretch of rusty track clashed with, no, insulted its location—a mechanical ode to man's folly, its horror echoing into infinity. The trees' shadows played cat-and-mouse on the rocky ground scattered with thousands of needles, spilled like so many tears by the garden's conifers. The bolder branches brushed the steel. The chill of winter was gradually giving way to the warm herald of spring. Birdsong wafted on a welcome breeze.

The agent didn't know the names of the trees. Sadness overwhelmed him. By what irony could he name the most insignificant component of a gun and be so ignorant of the natural habitat that had protected him so long? It was the price he had to pay for absolute devotion to his mission.

Pulling his knees up under his chin, gazing at the single car that symbolized so many more, giant Eytan was reminded of his insignificance. By his actions, however, he contributed to keeping the memory alive. Knowing and so never forgetting. Understanding and so never repeating. The Garden of the Righteous made him strong, consoled him when his task seemed insurmountable. Nobody could bring back the victims, but he had the power to punish their persecutors. For many years, he had hunted down and eliminated the scum. Like it or not, in more than one respect, Eytan Morg belonged to history. It gave his tragedy meaning. It had to have meaning. For the sake of those who died. For the sake of generations to come.

Deutsche Reichsbahn, München, 11689. A cattle car. How many terrified humans had been packed into the death trains? The number wasn't enough to grasp the agony. You had to feel it, experience the pressure of the tangled, crumpled bodies, hear the children sobbing, crushed against the legs of incredulous adults. In terror, the air fled, escaping toward a freedom those wretches would never know again.

The odious vehicle loomed over a cliff, pointing toward the precipice. Eytan knew pain and drew from it the remorseless strength to go on. Giving up would be like killing the martyrs of the Jewish nation and all the other victims of the holocaust a second time. How he hated himself for not being able to cry.

The husky voice of a chain smoker jerked him out of his reverie. "The farther backward you can look, the farther forward you are likely to see." Grave and deep, the words seem to rise from the soil. The man approached and stood behind the seated giant, who replied, without taking his eyes off the car, "Churchill knew and understood everything. I sometimes think he must have been seeing the world from the sky to have so much perspective."

"He saw it through the bottom of a glass. How are you, my friend?" The agent rose, dusting off his combat pants. He peered at the old man for signs of fresh wrinkles on his rugged face. At every one of their rare meetings, the passing of time seemed etched deeper in his features. Aged sixty-five, the scholar looked eighty. But under his bushy white eyebrows, his small blue eyes were as alert and piercing as those of any curious child.

"Fine. As always," said Eytan. "And you, Eli?"

"Better. As long as the doctors stay away from me. If you listen to them, I'm already dead. But old branches are the toughest, aren't they, my friend?"

"Don't I know it!"

Eli reached out and grasped Eytan's shoulder. Physical contact with the giant was the privilege of the keeper of Mossad's archives. "How did your mission in Iceland go?"

"Kurt Wetenhauser won't need dialysis three times a week anymore," Eytan replied tersely. Eli Karman dug into the pocket of his black pants and drew out a pack of cigarillos. Eytan clucked in disapproval. Grinning, his friend made a show of lighting it and gently exhaling a long blast of smoke. "Physical intervention, Agent Morg?"

"Violence has no place in the Garden of the Righteous. Nor has smoking." Eli's smile faded. "Why do we always meet here, Eytan? Why do you have to torture me?"

"I like it here. I am myself here. Whole. Like nowhere else on earth. I remember who I am."

"I understand. So, Wetenhauser, one of the butchers of Dachau, is no more. Pity we couldn't bring him to trial."

"He gave me no choice." Eytan threw a pebble and watched it skitter down the arid slope, bouncing off the rocks.

"Naturally. They all fear a trial more than death. Their logic will always be a mystery to me."

"They're monsters, Eli. We can never understand them."

"Don't fall into that trap, Eytan. The butchers are human beings, no more, no less. Seeing them as anything else would amount to ducking our responsibility as a species. That's why we prefer to take them alive. In order to expose their true, horrific nature. Ours."

"You haven't rubbed shoulders with them as I have. You're right, I know that. But being convinced they're monsters stops me slipping into fatalism with no way back. I want to believe in goodness. I've known it. It saved me. Allow me to believe it's anchored in the human soul. Allow me to hope that evil is the exception."

Eli Karman took a deep breath. He motioned toward the trees. "The Garden of the Righteous testifies to that. But I didn't come here for a philosophical debate, Eytan. I fear that your services are required once more."

"What's it about this time?"

"One of our agents in London was contacted by the Brits over some kind of archive trafficking at MI6. In recent months, a mysterious buyer has been acquiring confidential documents on contacts between the British secret service and the *Abwehr*, German military intelligence. Apparently, the officer in charge of the World War II files, which are of little interest to the British government now, has a bank account in Luxemburg. Large sums have been wired to it. As soon as Mossad has identified the source of the funds, you will go to meet the buyer to learn his motives. You will use all means necessary."

"If you thought he was a collector, you wouldn't ask me to intervene. Somebody high up thinks this is serious, right, Eli?" Eytan had known Karman too long. He could interpret every twitch of the old man's features. He'd never seen his superior look so horribly ill at ease.

"Certain documents concern secret SS operations at Stutthof camp. Does that ring a bell?" Over half a century since the fall of the Third Reich, the world had begun a new millennium, and yet history continued to repeat itself with a morbid stammer. Eytan looked down and spat out a sad laugh. So much suffering, so many wounds, only to see the ghosts of the past hold on and resurface. He clenched his jaw and then his fists. How could anyone keep their faith in humanity?

CHAPTER 22

Buffy's climbing the walls. I suppose crossing the Atlantic and escaping at least two killers—I have no idea how many were in the car that went boom—all for some accounting spreadsheets could cause some frustration.

"Crap, damn and shit!" Exasperation even.

"One hundred and twenty pages of incomprehensible figures. I don't believe it! We risked our lives for some stupid numbers and a crappy box. What the hell am I going tell Bernard? I have to call him in ten minutes."

She flops angrily on the bed, head in hands. That's the third time in an hour.

Pissed off, she scares me. Sprawled on the bed, she turns me on. I don't know why, but she does. Even so, I share her frustration. Traveling thousands of miles—not to mention fighting off all those attackers—for reams of cryptic figures leaves a sour taste. Looks like we're headed home to hand all this over to the CIA's number crunchers. I wouldn't be surprised if the investigation drags on for months. In a word, we're screwed.

Meanwhile, my mother's murderer is still on the loose. I can't bring myself to believe my dad brought us over here as some kind of sick joke. There's only one cynic in the family, and that's me. The documents lie in a pile on the bed, next to my cute little blonde. I lean over, pick them up and flick through them. Jackie's hot, but she's no auditor.

Slumped on the couch, pen in hand, I go through one page after another for five minutes.

The crybaby deigns to tune back into the world. "I have to call Bernard. What are you doing?"

"Reading. Isn't it obvious?"

"Forget it. We'll ask Bernard to get some experts to take a look at them."

Silly girl. "Actually, this is my specialty."

"What?"

"Account analysis. That's what I do. But to study these figures, I need some silence. If you could hit the mute button, you'd do us all a favor."

She gets up, brushes the hair off her face and comes over. "This jumble of numbers makes sense to you?"

She's trying my patience. "I'm a trader. I made a fortune making sense of jumbles of numbers, as you put it. Weapons and hand-to-hand combat are your line of work. Transactions and profit and loss are mine. Capone went to Sing Sing for tax evasion, remember. Guns don't solve everything."

She perks up and sits cross-legged on the bed, looking at me with a big grin. "Well, what have you found?"

"For now," I sigh, "major transfers of funds between bank accounts in Virginia, California and D.C. Tens of thousands of dollars every time. At least thirty recipients. The cash comes from several sources in Argentina, Brazil, Germany and Japan. From early this year through late June, so the last ones are pretty recent. I'll jot down the names of the recipients."

"I'll text Bernard to ask for a little more time."

I nod. A good idea, at last. "A lot more time. We have another problem. After the transfers of funds, there's a complete balance sheet for the first half of 2010. Companies buying up colossal amounts of chemicals.

The names mean nothing to me, but we should be able to track them down online."

"How colossal?"

"Hundreds of millions of units over a six-month period. If those kinds of volumes were normal, I think we'd know... You idiot, Jay! You total idiot!"

"Jeremy, hello..."

"Yes. Sorry, Jackie. What a prick I am!"

"You didn't know?"

"Thanks, pumpkin." Jackie's cheeks flush. She coos like a high school student who just got an A.

"The chemicals. I know why the quantities are so huge."

"How come, Mr. Smartypants?"

"Simple. I bought a ton of stock in pharmaceutical firms earlier this year. They were receiving gigantic orders and needed investment capital fast. Their stock price hasn't stopped rising since. So I know who's selling. And finding out who's buying will take one phone call. We have our lead. But why was my father so interested in these companies? And what's it got to do with the swastika on the key? Which opens what, by the way? It's hard to see where all this goes. I have another fifty pages to go through. In a couple hours, when I'm done, I'll make my calls."

Jackie lets out a low whistle. Admiration tinged with mockery. I don't care, I'm the best.

"Bernard told me you were good at what you do. I'm impressed. You have two hours to get the juice, and then we call him up. Get to work, sweet cheeks."

I've got my hands on a loose thread. Will I be able to unravel the entire cloth?

CHAPTER 23

The sounds coming through his headphones amused Eytan. Dean's baby spy was very entertaining, and Jeremy was showing talent. They were clearly caught up in this as victims, not criminals. The baddies hadn't been very efficient so far. But that wouldn't last. The closer they got to the truth, the bigger the obstacles and the more acute the danger would become. Eytan knew this from long experience, and this mission wouldn't be an exception to the rule.

The suction cup microphone on the wall between the two rooms relayed the tiniest ruffling of papers with astonishing clarity. Digital technology had revolutionized not only mass culture, but also the espionage trade. In fact, most mainstream hardware started out as a military application. Eytan always had the latest hi-tech gadgetry well before Joe Public had even heard of it.

He made the most of a momentary silence to try to fit what he had learned with the information already at his disposal. The puzzle began to take shape. It all made sense. But how? By what aberration were echoes of a painful past, an indelible scar on the whole of humanity, resonating in the present, seventy years later?

Eytan removed his headset, got up and pulled on a khaki shirt. He pulled the tight sleeves down over his repulsive forearms. He trudged into the bathroom and leaned forward to inspect his reflection in the mirror.

Freshly shaven, the color of his facial hair remained totally undetectable. His smooth complexion and perfectly symmetrical features were those of a thirty-year-old. For several long minutes, he gazed at himself with growing nausea.

He felt his phone vibrating in one of his pants pockets. Grabbing it, he read the message he had been hoping for since speaking to Eli ten minutes earlier. *New data on server. Read and acknowledge. Permission to continue with phase two. End of message.*

The fun was just beginning.

§ § §

"Jeremy, not only is Bernard going to be going ballistic, but we'll never get on a flight tonight if you don't wrap this up in five minutes."

I take a last series of notes. Hang up. Three calls for all that information. Good value. "OK, Jackie. I've got all I need. It's absolutely wacko."

"Talk." She sits down next to me.

"Here goes. In January, several pharmaceutical companies placed orders for millions of units of prod-ucts needed to make vaccines—basically, diluents, stimulants and additives. My father's figures alone de-tail transactions involving five hundred million units."

"That sounds enormous."

"Not if you take into account the population of developed countries. Until now, it never struck me as crazy. Not anomalous, at least. I called some guys I know in the city, guys I work with every day. The accounts of the major labs' suppliers are going through the roof. They spread orders across different companies and periods to keep it from drawing attention. If you add the volumes ordered in the last six months to the figures for January, you hit two billion doses. Now that is crazy."

"Crazy a lot?"

"Crazy staggering, Jackie. Especially since no health scare has necessitated the mass production of vaccines since the start of the year."

"Wrong."

The deep voice comes from the doorway. Like two synchronized swimmers, Buffy and I spin around. I knew it. I don't know why, but I knew it. Baldy stands there, hands in pockets. Wearing the same duds as when we met in New York. Jackie draws and points her gun at him. "Freeze! Not very smart, showing up unarmed. Especially a pro like you."

There's a mocking, vengeful edge to her voice. The guy seems to rub everyone the wrong way. Even so, the threat doesn't seem to worry him. In fact, he smiles.

"Hands up!" Jackie orders. His hands slip out of his pockets and rise toward the ceiling. That twinkle in his eye isn't a good sign. On the mark again! He unfolds his massive fingers. They're gripping a grenade. If Jackie fires, we all blow.

"I'm here to talk, not to pick a fight. Put your gun down. I don't mean you any harm." Jackie glances at me. Waits for my approval. I'm no secret agent or bodyguard. If the guy wanted to kill us, he would already have done so. With his wrong hand, too, for all I know.

I nod. Jackie lowers her gun hesitantly. The big clown has an annoyingly smug grin on his face. He slips the grenade back into his pocket. Morg—as Jackie called him on the phone with Bernard—ambles across the room and takes a seat on the couch, legs crossed, arms outspread.

"I was listening to you from next door. Good work, Jeremy. If you get bored with finance one day, I can get you a job with Mossad, no problem."

"Why not? As long as the salary isn't paid in knuckle sandwiches."

Jackie glances at me from the corner of her eye and frowns. I love that pretty face.

The Jolly Green Giant seems to have a better sense of humor. "I wasn't supposed to run into you. Just protect you. That's why I decked you. Sorry." He should be. My nose will remember our meeting for a long time.

Jackie chimes in. "Why did you say 'Wrong' when Jay said there had been no health scares?"

Morg takes his arms off the back of the couch and leans toward us. "Don't you read the newspapers?"

CHAPTER 24

Eytan takes the pile of complimentary newspapers off the coffee table. He rapidly flips through the pages until he finds the article he's looking for.

"Here we are. International section of today's *London Times*. '*The situation in Mexico is causing serious concern in the scientific community. The number of deaths linked to a new and particularly virulent strain of influenza has increased dramatically in recent weeks. The virus causes severe diarrhea, leading to dehydration. According to authorities, an estimated 2,000 people have died, and the number is rising. The incubation period seems much shorter than other influenza strains. A delegation from the World Health Organization is due to arrive in Mexico City, and credible sources are talking of widespread quarantine measures.*' I'll spare you the reporter's half-assed analysis of the geopolitical consequences," Morg concludes, lobbing the paper at my feet.

"So there is a health scare," Jackie sighs with a frown.

"It's better that way. At least, now we know what the vaccines are for." From the way they look at me, I figure I've said something stupid. "What?" I splutter.

"Labs order chemicals that will enable them to produce tons of vaccine just a few months before a particularly virulent epidemic starts, and you find that reassuring?"

Maybe they have a point.

"Hold on, before you crank up your conspiracy theories, remember there are pharmaceutical watchdogs and epidemiologists all over the world. There are even tighter controls than on many other sectors. Those guys just had great intuition. I'm not convinced."

Before Morg can reply, Jackie intervenes. "Before debating the ins and outs, maybe you should tell us who you are, why you're protecting Jay and on whose orders."

Short and to the point. Love it.

"My name is Eytan Morg. I work for Metsada, a unit within Mossad. To be even more precise, I'm a Kidon agent."

"Kidon?" That earns me more appalled looks. Apparently I should know.

"Kidon is a subunit created in the early seventies to conduct covert operations. The general public learned of it when Spielberg made *Munich*."

Now she's talking to me like I'm stupid. "Sorry, Jackie. Never saw it."

She goes on, "Kidon is the abduction and execution unit of the Israeli secret service. The name means bayonet in Hebrew. At the CIA, we study their techniques. Generally, they work in teams of four. Three men and a seductive woman if the target is a man. So, Agent Morg—Kidon Morg, I should say—where are your colleagues?"

"I have the peculiarity and privilege of working alone," he replies serenely.

Jackie's on a roll. "How do you know Bernard Dean?"

"I met him as part of a cooperation program between our two countries. That information is irrelevant to the current situation."

"Why make your entrance right now?"

This time, Eytan Morg seems to hesitate a moment. "For the very good reason that we need to work together with our cards on the table if we want to survive."

"What guarantee do we have you won't eliminate us once the mission is over?"

Good question!

"Mossad has nothing to gain by your deaths. You don't have many options. You can team up with me and benefit from my skills. Or you can go it on your own and then..."

He doesn't need to finish his sentence. He's made his point. An awkward silence ensues as we face off stonily. I wouldn't say no to a smoke—it must be the stress. The dilemma of a secret agent: Kill or be killed. Simple and cruel. I see now why Dad left home. How can you lead a normal life without compromising your family? A thought comes to mind. "Eytan? Could you answer Jackie's question? Why is Kidon protecting me? Why did you rescue Jackie in that alley?"

"My superiors appear to think that you have information that could lead us to a major enemy. Hence my intervention." He glances at the tiny blonde. "As for Agent Walls, you were safely in the bank, so when I saw those guys tailing her, it seemed like a good idea to do something."

Buffy nods her appreciation. Great. I have my own Mossad nanny. Party time.

"Would you mind telling us the whole story?" asks Jackie, as pragmatic as ever.

She brings out a hot sweat in me.

"You're right. I should explain, but it'll take some time. Can we take a look at the contents of the box first? I wouldn't be surprised if they corroborated a hypothesis that will make my explanations even clearer."

The box. I'd forgotten all about it. I grab it and remove the brown paper wrapping.

Eytan suddenly leans closer. We have in front of us a tiny, very scary-looking black box.

CHAPTER 25

Like a man possessed, the Israeli agent launched into a full-on history lesson. "In April 1945, Hitler stripped Himmler of all his duties after he was revealed to be negotiating with the Allies through the vice president of the Swedish Red Cross. The SS chief promised not to speed up executions in the concentration camps and to allow humanitarian organizations to send in food. In return, he hoped to avoid prosecution and obtain a position in Germany's post-war government. But the Allies rebuffed him, and who could blame them?

"After Hitler's suicide, Himmler tried in vain to join Admiral Dönitz's provisional government. Dönitz hated Himmler and sent him packing. In desperation, Himmler fled toward Austria wearing an eye patch and disguised as a sergeant major in the Secret Military Police. He was arrested at a British checkpoint on May 22, 1945. Ironically, Himmler's false papers aroused the Tommies' suspicion because they were unusually pristine and complete.

"As the Allied powers were spying on each other, a Canadian agent, John Stewart, had infiltrated the British unit. He discreetly made himself known to Himmler. When the *reichsführer-SS* realized he had been unmasked, he once more tried to negotiate. His talent for manipulation nearly saved his life. Secretly, he gave Stewart a key decorated with a swastika, which opened a safe that contained top-secret SS files.

It was Himmler's last bargaining chip. Scared of being seen with Himmler, however, Stewart disappeared with the key in his pocket.

"Himmler was brought in to see a doctor for a routine check-up. Despite his disguise, he was recognized by one of the guards. Cornered and in an attempt to obtain an interview with British secret service, Himmler gave the guards a small black box no bigger than a cigar box, engraved with the death's head symbol of the SS. Everybody ignored him. The check-up began. Seconds later, the prisoner screamed 'I am Heinrich Himmler' and bit into a cyanide capsule. He died betrayed, stripped of power and rejected on all sides. Poetic justice, perhaps, but the punishment hardly seemed to fit the crimes.

"Shortly afterward, the key flew to Canada with its new owner. The box was deposited in the MI6 archives with tons of documents seized from occupied Germany." This box. This key. Three pairs of eyes converged on the unnerving little box. Two initials in Gothic script flanked the embossed skull. H.H. Heinrich Himmler.

"What can be in there? It's tiny," Jackie said, mesmerized.

"As they say, there's only one way to find out," Jeremy replied eagerly. He inserted the tiny key into the lock. A spring clicked. The lid popped open.

"Shit!" Jeremy took out a black-and-white photo that had yellowed with age. "That's all there is," he murmured. The blurred photo showed a slim, ageless man in a white coat gripping the shoulders of a child who looked like he was somewhere between six and eight, head shaved, wearing a striped concentration camp uniform. The smug smile of the scientist contrasted with the child's eyes, which contained all the despair in the world. It was impossible to say if the child was a boy or a girl.

Jeremy handed the photo to Jackie. Lips pursed, she ran her fingers over it.

Eventually, it was Eytan's turn. Jaw clenched, he stared at it in silence. "Viktor Bleiberg," he sighed.

"Sorry?"

Eytan cleared his throat. "The man in the white coat is Professor Viktor Bleiberg, one of the worst criminals of World War II."

"Never heard of him." Jeremy glanced quizzically at Jackie for any reaction. She slowly shook her head.

"He died in an explosion in 1942," continued Eytan. "The Nazis did all they could to erase any trace of his existence." He flipped the picture over. "A sentence in German and a series of figures."

"We'll need a translator," Jeremy declared, slapping his thighs.

"False prophets make only self-fulfilling prophecies. That's what it says."

"You speak German?" Jeremy asked in amazement.

"I speak French, English, Hebrew, Polish, Russian, German and a little Spanish. I'm sure you feel smarter now that you know that."

Put in his place, Jeremy rolled his eyes and clammed up.

"The code was added later," Eytan went on. "It's not the same ink, and the handwriting is more contemporary. And from the three names, I deduce it's a message from Daniel Corbin. Jackie, do these codes remind you of anything?"

The two agents pored over the scribbled message.

JEREMY
DANIEL J.
ANN

18791411287279141111101125162725261125
12111627162221261112262122162526261210251
22726

DLIH

"Yes, it looks like a numeric key code. They're not necessarily complicated, but they can be a pain in the ass when you don't have the key. Which we don't."

"I could send it to my people for decoding, but I've been ordered to cease transmissions, and we have no time to lose."

"I'll talk to Bernard about it when I next speak to him," concluded Jackie.

Jeremy grabbed a pen and piece of paper, copied out the coded message and slipped the paper into his pants pocket. He unfolded the road map that had been in the safe-deposit box with the spreadsheets. A red arrow with a scribbled street name and number made any hypothesizing redundant.

"My father wrote down an address in Zaventem, Belgium. I guess we'll find answers to our questions there."

Eytan jumped up and headed for the door. "Pack your bags. Let's hit the road. We're headed for whatchamacallit on the map."

Jeremy glanced quizzically at Jackie. They should already have been on the flight home. Bernard was not going to be impressed. "Apologizing will be quicker than asking for permission we won't get. And I think our best option is to follow Eytan," answered the young woman.

Jeremy slapped his thighs and got up in turn. "OK, let's go. A trans-Europe trip with Kidon Airlines!"

CHAPTER 26

Our bags are ready. Jackie and I wait while Eytan empties a flight case of two silencers, three or four magazines and a cell phone, all of which wind up in various pockets of his combat pants. He also takes out a small black box the size of a cigarette case. With any luck, he smokes. If we outnumber Jackie in the car, I can smoke my ass off. He closes his case, presses the handle and twists it a quarter turn. Smoke filters out of the cracks.

"This tape will self-destruct in ten seconds, Mr. Phelps," I laugh. Alone. "Say, if you destroy everything on each mission, that's gotta add up for the Israeli taxpayer!" Long faces. Two days of all those I love or loved dying off around me. Humor is all I have left.

"Let's go. I'll tell you all I know in the car." Eytan grabs his army bag and opens the door. He closes it immediately. "Change of plan."

He drops his bag on the floor. Jackie does likewise. "What's going on?" she asks anxiously.

"Three guys about to enter your room. We need to take extreme measures."

"Releasing some tension won't do me any harm," says Jackie.

"OK. Three heads, three bullets. You want to prove I got you wrong?"

"Give me a gun. If I use mine, I'll have to fill out reams of paperwork when I get home."

She's not kidding. I have a question. "Don't you want to take one of them alive? They must know something."

"Smart. But I'll bet my jacket—and God knows I love my jacket—that they know nothing useful. Anyway, we have no time to interrogate them."

He lobs Jackie a gun. "Kill 'em."

"Hold on! What if they're cops?" Just asking.

"Cops don't use silencers."

Jackie nods to us and steps into the hallway. I don't like this. No, I'm definitely scared for her. "I hope you're not sending her to get slaughtered."

"I doubt it," he grins.

The door opens again. The gun is lobbed back from whence it came. Barely thirty seconds have passed. When Jackie has that expression on her face, you don't want to mess with her. "Let's get outta here," she says.

Eytan pockets the gun and nods. We exit.

In the hallway, I nudge our bedroom door open. One guy's strangely contorted on the bed. Another's sitting on the couch staring blankly at me. The last one's sprawled on his back on the floor, arms outstretched. Three guys, three bullets between the eyes. Impressive. The chambermaids will need a shrink.

Eytan comes over. He pulls a flat circular object out of his jacket pocket. He presses and twists the strange puck, then tosses it into the room. His big paw grabs my collar and shoves me forward. "C'mon, we have work to do." A muffled explosion echoes in the hotel room. I keep walking.

We quickly check out, pick up the rental and blow. Eytan programs the GPS with the address in Belgium, pulls into the Zurich traffic and heads for the freeway. As soon as we're out of the city, Jackie tries again. "I think you have some explaining to do. Don't you?"

As promised, Eytan begins his tale. "A little over six months ago, we received a request for assistance from senior people at MI6. A British agent had been taking World War II case files out of the archives at the Ministry of Defense. Certain officials make a little extra on the side by selling old reports to collectors or even writers. Given the space required to store dusty old files with no strategic importance anymore, a lot of department chiefs turn a blind eye to it or even skim off a commission. But in this instance, the Brits considered the documents sufficiently sensitive to ask for our help. I'll skip the details, but after a very persuasive chat with the incriminated agent, I found myself on the trail of a buyer in the United States."

"Persuasive? A chat like that with you is not something I'd relish," mutters Jackie.

"Me either," I add laconically.

"I'll leave you to your fantasies. Shortly afterward, I rocked up at a high-end beach house near Miami to meet a guy named Robert Delmar, a middle-aged American whose French parents had moved to Florida in the early seventies. Our checks on their son, a property developer with a small empire of beachfront buildings, came up blank. His father, however, provoked a frothing message from our intel department. Christian Delmar was a leading Vichy official in occupied France. Like many real or supposed collaborators, he held important positions in French post-war administrations, retiring in 1968 and emigrating to the States two years later. For the next decade, he was a consultant for a South American country specializing in the transfer of advanced technology. According to Bob, his father was an unscrupulous, cynical, manipulative bastard. The kid was born with a silver spoon in his mouth but struck out on his own to break free of his father's overbearing influence."

"He told you all that under duress?" Buffy asks with a disarming smile.

"Would you feel better if I told you our interview was cordial and friendly?" Eytan replies, teasing.

"Besides playing the shrink, did you find out anything?" For once, I'm the pragmatist.

"More than I ever expected. Hear me out. In 1985, Christian Delmar had a stroke that left him paralyzed from the waist down. Bob looked after him. His mother had died two years earlier. The old man held on another twenty years and died in 2009 at the ripe old age of one hundred and three, much to the relief of his son. Bob seemed trustworthy. I told him that his father was suspected of trafficking in classified information. His reaction was beyond my wildest dreams. He took me into his dad's office, which had been kept intact. It was Ali Baba's cave! The old man collected Third Reich memorabilia. The room was packed with flags, photos and reports, including the plans for some of the concentration camps."

"Nice." I feel a shiver running down my spine.

"You said it. But I know enough regular collectors to be sure that it wasn't just stuff gleaned here and there to feed some kind of sick fascination. Most often, it doesn't go much further than plates and silverware engraved with SS symbols. Sometimes things take a morbid turn. For example, a couple years ago, I came across a sicko who collected notepads and lampshades made of human skin. But in this case it looked more like a systematic analysis of the Nazis' industrial methods, techniques and innovations. Bob was good enough to let me explore. I spent a whole night in there going through Christian Delmar's personal notebooks. Two things in particular caught my attention. The first was an account in one of the notebooks of a visit to Landsberg Prison in 1924. Bonus question. Who was incarcerated there at that time?"

"I'd be inclined to say... Adolf Hitler?" Jackie gave a little top-of-the-class grin. "Exactly. Delmar and another guy—the notes referred to him as A.E.—met with the future führer to deliver a message from a mysterious consortium offering to help Hitler in his quest for power. You can imagine what a discovery like that means to Mossad."

"You're saying a secret organization helped the Nazis set the planet ablaze. You seriously believe that?" I'm dumbstruck.

"The question isn't whether I believe it or not. Even the most absurd lead must be investigated until it is proven true or false. On an assignment like this, acting on supposition is the surest way of screwing up."

"I see. And the second thing?"

"Delmar kept records of his transactions with various suppliers of his relics. The last entry mentioned my British acquaintance and, more important, the nature of the acquisition—a box that had belonged to Heinrich Himmler. There were scribbled notes all over the page. The old man's writing was impossible to decipher. It turned out the purchase had been made for a third party. Glancing through his records, I saw a similar entry. This time, it was for a key bought from a Canadian named Stewart, the guy who ran into Himmler just after his arrest. Again, the purchase was for the same third party."

"And the third party's name? Just trying to stay awake."

"Corbin." I'm not sleepy now.

"Dad?" My whole body feels like ten thousand volts are shooting through it.

"He features in Delmar's records under the name Jeremy Dean. Our intelligence department soon uncovered his true identity. If your father was Lieutenant General Daniel J. Corbin, ex-U.S. Air Force, who joined the CIA in 1986, abandoning wife and child in the process, then, yes, it was Dad."

"But my father wasn't some fanatical Nazi. At least, he wasn't when I knew him." I feel as sick as when I'm standing in front of my DB9 in the parking garage. I want to puke.

"Who said anything about fanatics? Your father didn't leave his family so he could get his kicks from a pent-up passion for fascism. Let me tell you the rest of the story, and you'll see. Bob allowed me to take anything I wanted, so I transmitted the information to my department head in Tel Aviv. The special relationship between the CIA and Mossad meant the answers came through fast, provoking more questions. Daniel joined the Agency on some kind of undercover assignment that necessitated a protection program."

"In plain English, please."

"Your father was a CIA undercover agent. He considered his mission sufficiently important to leave you and your mother. Undercover agents receive special treatment with regard to posting and reporting. If they think it necessary, they can disappear for one, five or even ten years and resurface only when it is possible or urgent to act. You find them in drug cartels, terrorist organizations and so on. It's not an easy sacrifice to make. Often, they can't reintegrate into society. Of course, it's impossible to know what organization Daniel was infiltrating or hoping to infiltrate. However, our contacts informed us of a problem with your dad's handler."

"His handler?"

Jackie chimes in, quoting from Espionage 101. "That's what we call the operative to whom the undercover agent transmits information. What was the problem?"

"Let's just say, heaps of cash coming in, heaps of data on Corbin going out. Get the picture?" Eytan grins smugly. The guy likes sounding off. I want to know more, but Jackie beats me to the draw.

"The handler sold his agent?"

"Not only that. I asked the Yanks to be allowed to clean up the problem in return for a detailed report on what I found out and a promise to be discreet. The guy's name was William Pettygrow. I winged it by making contact with him in a hunters' bar near Langley. After a few beers, I told him I'd be interested in anything on your father. He didn't even act surprised and told me a woman had already bought some information from him the week before. Two months before he retired, he thought putting together a little nest egg by selling intel on an insignificant agent wouldn't get him into any trouble. Eventually, he told me of a message from Bernard Dean to your father, confirming that a safe-deposit box in Switzerland had been leased. Corbin never received the message."

"And Pettygrow?"

"For a reason I can't fathom, his attitude toward me became distinctly frosty. The previous buyer must have warned him off. Now he's compost for conifers somewhere in Virginia. I can't tell you where—it depends on the prevailing winds. That's all I know."

CHAPTER 27

Another nicotine break. To my surprise, Eytan smokes one with me. He claims to be an occasional smoker, cigars mostly. I look at him—huge, well-built, good-looking—and wonder what he was like as a boy. How does a kid grow up to be an assassin? How does he take the step from regular human being to cold-blooded killing machine? His angular features give no insight into the boy he once was. And yet, in this deserted and desolate rest stop in the middle of nowhere, I glimpse fragility. He lets the mask slip, and I like that.

Jackie gets out of the car, yawns and stretches languorously. She sees us and smiles. I glow. A big mitt grasps my shoulder.

"She's a beautiful woman. Funny and smart."

The remark catches me off guard, but I guess it was supposed to. Anyway, in the wasteland of my life, Eytan is the closest I have to a friend right now. So I forget my usual defense mechanisms and fess up. "I think she's wonderful."

Eytan savors every drag of the cigarette, blowing smoke high in the sky. He turns to me and smiles. "She fights well, she's brave, but she has a cruel lack of experience."

"I don't care!" My outraged tone makes him laugh, affectionately almost. He leans closer and whispers, "Jay, I know how you feel."

"You have somebody?" He flicks his butt away, stares into space, then heads over to Jackie. I won't get an answer to my question.

§ § §

Eytan decided it was Jackie's turn to drive while he rode shotgun. All Jeremy could do was sprawl in the comfortable backseat and slip into an agitated sleep.

As the road raced by beneath their wheels, the Israeli veteran grilled the CIA apprentice on combat techniques and protection protocols. A full-on oral exam. While Jackie answered confidently without missing a beat, Eytan sensed sweat beading on his brow. As discreetly as possible, he slipped his shaking hands into his pockets. "Jackie, pull over at the next gas station, will you?"

"But we just stopped," she sighed. "You need the little boys' room?"

"You could say that."

Twenty or so miles up the road, the Lexus pulled off the highway, past the gas pumps, which were deserted so late at night and pulled up outside the cafeteria. Eytan leaped out and hurried inside.

Jackie couldn't resist the temptation to shake Jeremy. He woke with a start, yelling, "Budding love!" He was handsome with a sense of humor that sometimes made her laugh and often didn't. She had to admit, he was irresistible.

"Eytan's making a pit stop. If you need to join him, go ahead. I'm going to call Bernard."

Jeremy sat up and stretched. "Good, I want a word with him. I'll take a leak afterward."

Sometimes he wasn't quite so irresistible. Jackie grabbed her cell phone and hit last-number redial. She turned the speakerphone on. After three rings, the phone picked up. "It's me, sir. Things have been heating up. We're on our way to Belgium. I'm using a stop to touch base and pass on the information Morg gave us."

"Good evening, Jacqueline. Very kind of you to call." Jackie and Jeremy looked at each other in surprise as a strange humming sound and a woman's voice came out of the phone.

"Who are you?"

"You can call me Elena. I'm getting a slight echo, so I presume that other people are listening in. Jeremy Corbin or Eytan Morg or maybe both of them?"

"Put Bernard Dean on," Jackie ordered with a tremor in her voice.

"I fear that's impossible, sweetie. I lodged a bullet in the back of his head. Rest assured, he didn't feel a thing. A quick, clean hit. Just like the one on Jeremy's mother."

Jackie stifled a scream. She froze in her seat, torn between stupor, anger and grief. Jeremy leaned closer. "Listen up, bitch. We're gonna put an end to your dumbass project, and I'll break your neck with my bare hands. But I won't lie, it won't be quick or clean."

A burst of laughter came through the line. "Mister Corbin, this isn't personal. It's business. Anyway, I'd be curious to see you try. Trust me, you'll soon get your chance. If you survive our next little skirmish, of course.

Speaking of which, you shouldn't stop so often. Your lead on our representatives diminishes by the minute."

Jackie snapped out of it and hung up. A silent tear trickled down her face. She removed the SIM card from the cell phone and handed it to Jeremy. "Go get Eytan, and toss that down the toilet. Tell him to lose his card too." Jeremy nodded and jumped out of the car to look for the giant.

Alone in the car, Jackie drew her gun and checked the clip. She was sure the humming she heard over the phone was the sound of airplane engines. As she was about to turn the key in the ignition, headlights lit up her rearview mirror.

§ § §

I cut through the store, watched by the bovine eyes of the clerk slumped behind the counter, who's shamelessly reading the big-tits special issue of a porn magazine. Apparently he isn't expecting a busy night. The refined atmosphere is only heightened by Aerosmith's "Sweet Emotion" blasting from the loudspeakers. I walk past three coffee machines that have seen their last customers for the day.

I have to get my head together. Bernard's death has frazzled my brain. I last saw my father more than twenty years ago. I visited my mother maybe ten times a year. Bernard was there for me every day. I really loved the guy. He was my true family.

A long hallway takes me past tables covered with remains left by the last visitors—plastic cups, breadcrumbs, sandwich wrappers. The doors at the rear of the vast room are padlocked with heavy chains. To my right is a hallway with signs on either side pointing to the men's and ladies' restrooms. All the lights are on. If gas stations at all the rest stops on the continent switched off just half of the lights in the hallways leading to their bathrooms, they'd save considerable energy and boost their bottom lines. Which would impact positively on their stock prices. Professional reflexes are hard to shake off. People never change.

The pale blue tiles are oppressive. The heady odor of toilet detergent assaults my nostrils. The only sound comes from water trickling down the porcelain of four urinals on the right-hand wall. The same number of mirrors and sinks are on the opposite wall. And facing the door are three closed stalls, the throne rooms. To be used only as a last resort and at your own peril.

"Eytan?" No response. I listen attentively for signs of plumbing work in progress. Nothing. I call his name again. Still no response. Needs must when the devil drives. I hunker down to peek under the doors. There's no point yelling like an idiot if he's not in there.

Middle door first. Bull's-eye! Weird, though. He's been in there at least two minutes, and his pants aren't around his ankles. And he's not answering me. Something's up. I hope nothing's happened to him. I head into the stall on the right, step up on the toilet and peer over the partition. For one fleeting moment, I'm scared this will get me a bullet between the eyes.

Eytan's sitting on the can. I make a racket clambering up and keeping my balance, but he doesn't budge an inch. In his left hand, he holds an empty syringe. He turns and looks up at me in painfully slow motion. My gaze collides with his. His pupils are dilated, his complexion is waxy, and his lips are blue. The sight of him makes my blood freeze. I topple off the toilet, nearly twisting my ankle. Before I bail, I dump Jackie's

SIM card in the john and pull the flush. Shit! Our lives depend on a junkie. I don't hang around. He's out of action for a while. Maybe Jackie will know what to do with the dope fiend. Problems are piling up so fast I can't think. Everything's slamming together in my head, and fear of a gruesome end overwhelms me. I head back. A move that saves my life.

In the big empty cafeteria, I hear two gunshots outside. Instinctively, I hunch over. Good thinking. The third gunshot blows the windows out of the back doors. Two goons like the ones who chased me in my building burst in, aiming their guns at me. No time to think twice. I dive through the shattered window, landing on the broken glass and asphalt as more shots ring out and sparks fly around me. I haul myself up and run like crazy for the trees bordering the rest stop. The shouts behind me convince me I'm being followed. Screw Eytan, he can look after himself. What a stupid idea to shoot up at a time like this!

Amid the chaos, another Aerosmith song, "Living on the Edge," comes to me. A curious coincidence, but that just about sums it up.

CHAPTER 28

Jackie thanked her lucky stars and the landscape architects for insisting on leaving wooded areas around highway rest stops. The copse of trees behind the gas station was a welcome refuge from the three assholes intent on putting a bullet in her. Bent double, she picked her way through the trees, looking for the one offering the most protection. Fortunately, the three men weren't toting automatics. They could have sprayed bullets into the woods at random and blown her away. But now a game of hide-and-seek was developing, and since she was a little girl that had always been one of Jackie's favorite games.

She had two choices: keep moving and hope they would play into her hands or hide and wait for the chance to pick them off one by one. She squatted against a tree trunk to get her breathing under control and make her decision.

Jackie crawled through the undergrowth, relying on her size and speed to work in her favor if she ran into anybody. Flat on her belly, she spotted a foot and took careful aim. She fired twice. The man collapsed on the ground, screaming. At the very least, the bullets had broken his foot or, with a little luck, ripped his toes off. The wounded man's screams gave Jackie a buzz. In the unlikely event that he survived tonight, the guy would be disabled for life. When the thirst for revenge grabs you, that knowledge can be very satisfying. Two more opponents to eliminate. Jackie concentrated hard.

The rustle of branches on suits gave Jackie precious clues to their whereabouts. Suddenly, twigs cracked behind her. She spun round, gun in both hands and fired, aiming by instinct. Alert, her muscles coiled, she spotted her second target. Short hair, square jaw, brown eyes, early thirties, good-looking. The gun he leveled at Jackie made him less attractive. As did the red stain spreading across his white shirt level with his solar plexus. He swayed for a few seconds, then toppled onto Jackie, who rolled just in time to avoid being crushed by two hundred pounds of dead meat. Another one down.

§ § §

Damn floodlights! The parking lot is empty, and in the harsh light I'm a sitting duck. I run like mad, convinced that every step will be my last. I glance around to see if they're closing on me. Strangely, there's nobody there. Two gunshots ring out. The tables and stone stools for travelers to eat their ready-made meals are bordered by this charming copse of trees. In the daytime, kids chase each other, and dogs shit here gaily. But tonight, especially for me, the rest stop has become a shooting range. Seeing the muscular guy peering into the trees with his back to me, I wouldn't be surprised if Jackie was somewhere in the undergrowth. Hopefully, she's not wounded. Or worse.

At top speed, I use a stool, then the table to launch myself at the guy. In the movies it looks great. The baddie doesn't see you coming and politely lets you land on him. In real life, the baddie hears you coming and ducks. I land in a heap on the ground. He hauls me up by the collar and rams the cold steel of his gun against the side of my head.

"Hands up! Now!" he hisses. I obey. I take a rabbit punch to the kidneys—an unpleasant way to get me moving toward the store I left at a sprint. I stagger back. Eytan on his cloud. Jackie MIA. Bernard dead. I feel very alone. I drag my feet because that's what you do. My escort shoves me because he's enjoying this. He didn't kill me, so they must want to talk to me. That's reassuring. The prospect of our upcoming chat, less so. I hope he's not as persuasive as Eytan.

We take a shortcut through the now empty door-frames into the cafeteria.

Broken glass crunches underfoot. No more Aerosmith. At the far end of the hallway, the corpse of the porniac clerk is sprawled among the sandwiches and candy. Standing next to the body, another goon waits for me. Outside, a BMW SUV idles, passenger door open. We pass the bathrooms. I hope they haven't found my favorite Israeli.

"Hit the deck, Jay!" I don't need to be told twice, dropping to the tiled floor immediately. Glancing around, I see my escort with a knife sticking out of his neck. Behind him, Eytan holds him tight. The poor guy tries to grab the knife with one hand. In vain. The agent seizes the other hand holding the gun and forces his prisoner's arm up. Pulling hard on the finger of the frantic puppet, Eytan opens fire. Once. The crashing sound in the store confirms a hit. Twice, to finish the job. The giant turns toward me. A sudden thrust of the knife drives the blade straight through the reluctant gunman's neck. Blood spurts from his mouth.

Tires squealing, the SUV speeds up. Eytan spins toward the back door and pulls out of his pocket a puck identical to the one he used in the Zurich hotel. The roaring engine gets louder, and the BMW hurtles past, the passenger door still open. The little black puck sails through the air and sticks to the back of the SUV. A shadowy figure hurries out of the trees and dives into the moving van. Eytan takes out his remote and hits the button. A ball of flames engulfs the rear of the BMW. The combination of the powerful explosion and its speed makes the SUV lift off like a rocket, as if swiped upward by a titanic force. The SUV flies up, flips over backward and lands on its roof.

Eytan's impressive build and bald head are silhouetted against the smoke and flames as he heads for the blazing vehicle after drawing a pistol equipped with a silencer as long as bounty hunter Josh Randall's sawed-off Winchester. I run after him, but the giant is totally oblivious to me. He keeps going, both hands on the gun held out in front of him.

Somebody squirms out the passenger door. I'd recognize that body anywhere. "Eytan, don't shoot! It's Jackie!"

He keeps going. Twenty paces ahead, Jackie crawls on all fours on the asphalt. She looks badly shaken, but not obviously wounded. She gets up with some difficulty and turns toward us. I can't really see her face, but her size and shape put the issue beyond doubt.

"Eytan?" Why won't he lower his gun, the jerk? Jackie backs up toward the wreckage of the car, staring incredulously at us. Eytan fires off a whole magazine. I can't breathe. Buffy instinctively ducks. Behind her, near the trees, a badly limping man has taken aim and is about to shoot her in the back. The volley of bullets blasts him through the branches and into a tree trunk.

"Jeremy, try shutting up when I'm taking aim. You distract me," he says with a wink in my direction. I gasp for breath. Jackie likewise. She comes over, covered in mud and soaked in sweat. Her leather jacket is singed.

"I honestly thought you were going to blow me away." She's been doing acrobatics in a burning car, and she laughs it off. This girl blows me away.

"Would I do a thing like that? Situation?" Eytan asks, deadly serious.

"Three enemy operatives. One shot in the trees. Another winged in the foot and finished off by you just now, kind sir. Plus the driver, whom I had knocked out prior to interrogation, but he's unlikely to be very talkative now. You two?"

Eytan holsters his impressive pistol. "They shot the clerk. One enemy dead in the store. Another outside the bathroom. Plus the car knocked out. Thank Christ, no civilians showed up. It would have been carnage."

I glance around me. A hundred-thousand-dollar car parked on its roof and smoking like a sausage on a barbecue. A few yards away, a corpse riddled with bullets hugging a tree. In the cafeteria, another body on a carpet of broken glass with a knife sticking out of its throat. Down the hallway, the sad sack who was working in the wrong place at the wrong time is sprawled side by side with the last of the commandos on a bed of chips and candy.

And the giant wacko thinks that's not carnage.

CHAPTER 29

We're making good time. The GPS estimates arrival in four hours. I didn't see anything of Switzerland. Shame, it's supposed to be pretty. I'd like to think I'll take in the sights next time. If there is a next time.

Jackie's asleep in the backseat, still dazed from Bernard's killing and the shootout. We're all taking it bad. Even Eytan Morg. They knew each other better than he's letting on. Maybe he'll tell us about it in his own sweet time. I hope so. His bathroom break hasn't made things simpler. He drives, eyes staring at the road ahead. Tough shit, I need to talk. "Besides work and getting high, what do you do all day?" No answer. You're out of luck, pal. I'm pigheaded. "The journey will seem shorter if we talk, don't you think?"

He sighs. "When I'm not on an assignment, I paint." I can't help laughing. "You think that's funny?"

"I'm picturing you on a stool with your palette and brush, gazing at a green valley or a snowy mountaintop. Sorry, but with your look and build, it's funny!"

"If you're just going to make fun of me, the trip is going to seem very, very long." He clams up.

"There's no harm in a little fun. OK, I'll stop," I snort, laughing even louder. Why do giggling fits always hit at inappropriate times?

"What about you? Besides driving home from clubs dead drunk, what do you do?"

Bastard. That's below the belt. On second thought, I guess I deserved it. "I try to survive. I thought about blowing my brains out, but I'm too much of a coward. So I drink. I smoke like a chimney. Every day, I destroy myself a little bit more."

"Suicide isn't a sign of bravery, but of giving up. We all make mistakes. You don't judge somebody by the number of blows they can give."

"What do you judge somebody by, Mr. Freud?"

"The number of blows they can take."

His words hit home. "You've taken a lot, right?" I ask. A long, long beat.

"More than you can ever imagine."

Why am I not surprised? This guy's been around the block. I'd bet my life on it. "How do you do it?"

"Pardon me?"

"Blowing guys away like that. How do you do it?"

"Who said it was easy?" He sighs heavily. A long awkward silence. My questions seem to carry Eytan onto a stormy sea whose crashing waves he'd do anything to avoid. I plow on.

"I saw you kill two guys in my building. Jackie told me you eliminated two more who ambushed her. And now the rest-stop massacre. No trembling, no hesitation. By my calculations, you've wasted eight guys in under twenty-four hours."

"I suspect the total is closer to ten—one every three hours since we met."

He glances at the dashboard clock. "Another hour, and I'll have to kill somebody else to keep up my batting average." Maybe Eytan thinks he can laugh this off. My frown disabuses him of the notion.

"Don't try to worm your way out of it. I repeat, how do you do it? I want an answer." Unintentionally, I raise my voice. "I need an answer!"

"Why? How will knowing help you? Am I your fantasy? Does death fascinate you or the idea of killing turn you on? Maybe it revolts you. Whatever. What do you expect me to say? Yes, I kill. Killing is my job. Watching over you is my mission. Count yourself lucky you're not my enemy."

"That's not an answer."

"For Christ's sake, what the hell is it to you?"

"I want to understand who you are. Are you surprised?"

Eytan suddenly steers the Lexus onto the shoulder, screeches to a halt and spins toward me. "Listen up, doofus. I lied when I told Jackie I work alone. I carry centuries of oppression on my shoulders. I have an army behind me. One hell of an army! Six million men, women and children exterminated in a few short years. Not to mention the gays, gypsies and other victims of hatred and ignorance. I stand between the wackos and the innocent. I kill so nobody will have to die. That's why I never tremble, I never hesitate, and I never regret. If I fail in my mission, the martyrs of the Shoah will have died in vain. Wolves lurk in the shadows. I smoke them out. If they still want to fight, I annihilate them. You want to know who I am, Jeremy? I am a rampart."

Silence. I'm impressed by the huge effort he has made to express himself calmly, without raising his voice. The gravity of his argument is enough. I fiddle awkwardly, head down, staring at my feet. Put in my place.

The car pulls away again. Jackie's still asleep. Imperturbable. Beautiful.

"What if Mossad had its own in-house Pettygrow?"

The question is provocative but not as dumb as it might seem. He nods. "Considering the apparent links between our enigmatic opponents and the Nazis, I can't imagine any of our people allying themselves with them."

"Of course. You're one big family, and you stand united against aggression, right?"

"I couldn't put it any better. Do you have any idea of the number of enemies the state of Israel has? Without unfailing solidarity, our country would lie in ruins," Eytan retorts with a hint of irony, trotting out the official line.

But I'm not a total chump. "Remind me, Agent Morg. Who killed Yitzhak Rabin?"

Got him! Eytan shoots me a sidelong glance. His jaw twitches. "In World War II," I add, "didn't some Jews willingly collaborate with the Nazis?" Slowly and painfully, he turns toward me. His features are drawn.

"They did, Jeremy. I know that better than anyone."

DAY 4

CHAPTER 30

BERLIN, MAY, 1945.

Andrei Kourilyenko couldn't believe his eyes. The typically laconic intelligence reports claimed thirty to seventy percent of Berlin had been destroyed, depending on the neighborhood. But where were the parts of the city that were intact? The German capital was like a film set with only the facades of bombed-out buildings still standing. The streets were littered with the stinking, rotting corpses of members of the *Volkssturm*, the last line of resistance composed of civilians and children.

The convoys trucking in Soviet administrative units traveled by night. In the headlights, Andrei glimpsed shadowy figures fleeing the Red Army uniforms. He heard gunshots in the ruins as indiscriminate punishment was wrought on the German people. They were paying a heavy, painful price. The millions killed by Operation Barbarossa would not be resuscitated by flattening Berlin and massacring its population. As if war were not sufficiently absurd already. As if the savagery of the victors could erase the barbarity of the defeated.

Sheer stupidity, he mused. Expressed out loud, the thought would have seen him hauled before a firing squad within the hour. Like many of his comrades, he recalled that Stalin shared Hitler's penchant for repression. Under both regimes, silence was the only method for extending one's life expectancy. Germany had its führer, the Soviets had a *vozhd*, a guide. The difference between them was a question of semantics.

Andrei lived hidden in the hushed corridors of scientific administration. All Sonya, his wife, and their young daughter knew of the conflict was what state propaganda wanted them to know. In Moscow, Andrei's job was to compile lists of scientists and translate their works into layman's language. Ten years at university and drawers full of diplomas ensured him a job. Losing an eye to a neurological disease spared him active participation in the war. His handicap advanced his career. In a terrifying world, he looked the part. Always immaculately dressed, his graying hair cropped short, he wore glasses with smoked glass concealing his missing right eye. He scared his colleagues. It was the ideal cover for a shy man and passionate lover of classical music and French literature. Such notoriously tsarist hobbies had to be kept absolutely secret.

Hunched in his seat in the black car, Andrei jumped when a woman ran frantically across the road, only just avoiding the speeding vehicle. He glimpsed her torn clothes and bare breasts. Two men chased after her. Rape on top of plunder and summary executions. Defeating the Nazis was one thing, but the blood spilled here wouldn't bring back the millions of Russian victims. As ever, the propaganda machine would gloss over the atrocities and turn reality into a hymn to Stalin's glory.

Andrei understood the thirst for revenge but had no desire to witness or be an accomplice to it. His presence here reflected another dimension of the war.

The rout and scattering of Nazi dignitaries marked the beginning of an international bidding war. The British, using MI6's extensive contacts in the *Abwehr*, were offering German scientists gilt-edged contracts, but they were nothing compared to the Americans' massively funded Operation Paperclip. For months, Andrei had tracked American attempts to spirit away leading German brains. Their biggest success so far had come three weeks earlier with the acquisition of Wernher von Braun, the rocket scientist, who left for the New World with much of his research team. Frothing with rage, Stalin had ordered Department 7 of the NKGB, the Soviet secret service, to round up the remaining scientists or face serious reprisals. Quite simply, for the unit's chiefs, failure would lead at best to a stay in Siberia, at worst, to the firing squad.

So that's how Andrei found himself in hell, amid mostly illiterate peasant soldiers. The Soviet Union wanted a coordinator with a scientific background. Why did they have to pick him? The convoy of three cars and two trucks continued through the ruins until it came within sight of the German parliament. Powerful spotlights stood on heaps of rubble, sweeping the ground and sky. The architectural splendor of the Reichstag proved no defense against the Red Army's shells. Andrei spotted a charred tree emerging from a mass of stone and steel. Glancing around, he saw the wreckage of a Messerschmitt, of which only the engine and propeller remained intact. He looked up and noticed the shell of the building's bombed-out dome. Unfortunately, approaching from the south, they couldn't see the flag raised there a few days earlier as a symbol of total victory. Three huge tanks were parked on the cratered plaza, which was covered with shards of glass from the gigantic windows blown out by the shelling.

The convoy pulled up behind the tanks. Andrei got out, relieved to get away from the taciturn driver, who had added to his boredom in the last few hours. Six men in uniforms, his personal escort, got out of the other two cars. Fifteen seconds later, seven cigarettes were lit almost simultaneously. A few minutes after that, the butts bounced off the ground at the soldiers' feet. Vulgar jokes about the fall of the Nazi regime were shared. Laughing at other people's problems helped them avoid issues closer to home that might provoke unease and suspicion.

Andrei thought back to the terms of his mission. The secret service would meet about twenty scientists and engineers at night outside the Reichstag. Salaries and perks would depend on the classifications that he alone would establish. His priorities, at the specific request of top brass, were rocket engineers, followed by armament specialists and the rest, who would be offered less comfortable packages. But in the current climate, less was better than nothing. The annihilation of Germany would, at least, compel the survivors to accept not very much at all, allowing the victors to sign people up cheaply. The recruits' level of implication in the Nazi regime or possible misdeeds mattered little. The thought chilled Andrei's blood. Revenge, liberty and ideals were already being sacrificed for potential profit. Churchill, Roosevelt, Stalin, de Gaulle—none of them escaped the hollow pragmatism of economic and military interests. A new world order would soon emerge. The battle for top spot would be fierce and technology-based.

Yelling cut short the commissar's musings. Outside the ravaged parliament building, about fifty armed soldiers were barking orders and brutally herding a huddled group of about twenty men, some of whom wore lab coats over SS or Wehrmacht uniforms, while others were in rags. All were trembling with fear. Except one, the youngest. He couldn't have been more than thirty. His impeccable civilian suit stood out in the desolation. Hands in pockets, the incongruous character stared at the gathering with surprising haughtiness.

Andrei and his escort climbed the steps toward the terrified group. "Gentlemen, please excuse our soldiers' rough manners. Rest assured that no harm will come to you. From today on, you are working for the Soviet Union. We will erase your relationship with the Nazi regime. You and your families will be accorded comfortable living conditions, as long as you perform your duties without complaint."

Andrei spoke nearly flawless German. Only a slight Russian accent betrayed his lack of practice. It was one of the advantages of childhood years spent in the Bavarian branch of his cosmopolitan family. His deliberately affable tone and fluent language had the desired effect. The captives relaxed.

"I will call out your names, and you will join the three cars parked at the bottom of the steps. An agent of the NKGB will inform you of the terms and conditions of your employment, remuneration and location. Each group will be taken by truck to a Soviet base. I must emphasize the exceptional nature of the opportunity being offered to you. Refusal to comply will result in your arrest, and you will have to answer for your acts before a court of law. Do I make myself clear?"

Nodding heads confirmed the message had been understood. Everything was going as planned, and the mission was proving less complicated than he had anticipated. The herd of sheep hardly had much choice.

Andrei began calling out names from his list. Scientists and engineers filed past in an almost cordial atmosphere. Andrei was thankful for the generosity of Stalin and his henchmen. Forcing these men to work under hard conditions would result in the loss of their expertise. Or send them into the open arms of the Western powers.

Gradually, the trucks parked a hundred yards away were filled until only one recruit remained, a chemist-geneticist about whom Andrei had virtually no information besides his glittering university career.

"Bleiberg, Viktor." The elegant young man strode forward.

"You studied with Professor Hahn. Very impressive. Radiation research—a sensitive subject. We will offer you the possibility to continue your work." They began to walk toward the trucks.

"I don't think so," Bleiberg replied without so much as a glance at Andrei.

"You'd rather face trial?" the Russian asked in a barely veiled threat.

"No. You see, I'm no longer at the experimentation stage, and other people require my services."

They paused. Their eyes locked as they stared each other down. "You are in our hands. Who will come for you now?"

Bleiberg cracked an evil grin and jutted his chin toward the convoy. "They will."

The commissar glanced around and felt sick. Corpses were sprawled around the cars and trucks. His escort lay in pools of blood. A dozen hooded men dressed in black from head to foot had guns trained on

Andrei's herd. Not the slightest sound had accompanied the massacre.

Andrei reached for his holster, but before he could draw, he felt the cold steel of a gun barrel nudging the side of his head. Bleiberg grinned at him. The scientist leaned closer and adjusted the commissar's uniform.

"I wish I could say that fortune played a mean trick on you. Alas, we cannot take fate into consideration. Allow me to salute the pertinence of the list you drew up despite the Americans beating you Soviets to the draw. They were quicker and smarter than you. But thanks to your expert analysis, Stalin was about to get his dirty hands on some eminent scholars, engineers and technicians."

Shaken to his bones, the Russian stammered, "You knew of the operation? You're an American agent?"

Bleiberg pressed his lips to the Russian's ear. "I'm a member of an international organization for which borders, flags and patriotism have no meaning. When your list was communicated to us, I was struck by the intelligence of your selection. Excellent military choices and superb industrial vision."

"I suppose you're going to eliminate me now?"

"Eliminate you? You couldn't be more wrong, Kourilyenko. I am going to complete your mission."

Petrified since the start of their conversation, Andrei now looked on the verge of collapse. "I beg your pardon?"

Viktor Bleiberg grasped the dumbstruck commissar's right hand. "My dear commissar, I came here to recruit you."

CHAPTER 31

Zaventem, Belgium, Saturday.

The address scrawled on the map was on a narrow street lined with shops in the center of town. Intrigued, Eytan parked outside a pizzeria with a marquee in the colors of the Italian flag. At nearly four in the morning, downtown Zaventem was dead. Except for a couple of cars, there wasn't a soul to be seen. The street-lights seemed superfluous in this small, ghostly town. Stuck between the Ring, the freeway that connected Brussels to its outskirts, and the international airport, Zaventem was a charmless commuter town.

Jet lag and physical and nervous exhaustion had caught up with Jeremy. He'd been fast asleep for a good two hours. A big nudge from Eytan jerked him out of his slumber. Jackie was accorded a slightly less brutal awakening. Barely a minute later, the three of them were walking cautiously down the sidewalk, alert to the slightest movement. An ambush on a narrow street like this would be infinitely less manageable than the attack at the rest stop. The two agents stayed on either side of Jeremy. A car turned into the street. Eytan grabbed the trader's shoulder and dragged him into an alcove that housed an ATM. Jackie ducked behind a parked car, one hand on her revolver.

The Kidon agent's relaxed approach was history. Eytan sensed they were closing in on the truth, and nothing could be left to chance until the whole sinister business was over. The small red Toyota turned left at the first intersection. False alarm. They kept walking.

Outside No. 22, they stopped and exchanged incredulous looks when they saw the bookstore's highly evocative name, Deep Zone. In the windows, posters for manga showed futuristic heroines with alluring, if slightly exaggerated curves. Comic books and graphic novels formed a patchwork of colors, shapes and unlikely titles. The motto on the window proclaimed the store's ethos: *The Temple of the Imagination.* Which may have explained the presence of old Dungeons and Dragons game boxes. A curtain blocked off the inside of the store. Eytan checked the address on the map three times, backed into the road to confirm the number and glanced around until he found a sign with the street name on it. Clearly, he found it hard to accept that this paradise for overgrown teenagers could play a decisive role in the success of their mission.

Jeremy, on the other hand, was psyched, pointing to various role-playing games. Collector's editions from the nineteen eighties, he claimed, while inflicting on Jackie the complete history of a game he had been addicted to as a kid. Bemused, she nodded politely, silently praying that Eytan would quickly decide their next step.

"We're going in," Eytan said, leaning over the lock on the door. Jeremy almost squealed with excitement. Jackie thanked heaven for the respite from his geekish gushing. Fifteen seconds later, the lock's rudimentary mechanism yielded to the attack of a credit card in the skilled hands of the Israeli agent. He entered, peered at the frame and followed the wires to the switchbox above the door. The others didn't have to wait long for his expert conclusion. The so-called alarm had given up the ghost long ago. But it didn't seem likely that anybody would want to steal this stuff, anyway. The cash register, meanwhile, probably never held more than loose change.

With a sharp whistle, Eytan signaled Jeremy and Jackie to enter. Jackie stopped next to Eytan and imitated his hands-on-hips pose, staring at the narrow shop that stretched back maybe twenty yards. Huge shelves covered the walls. They were packed with an array of novels, comic books and figurines, from *Star Wars* to *Lord of the Rings*. Thousands of books. A thousand square feet maybe and as many documents as Mossad's complete archives.

"OK, we don't know what we're looking for and have, at a conservative estimate, a million pages to go through. Seven hours on the road to wind up here."

"Eytan, maybe we should see if there's a hiding place. That door must lead to the storeroom. C'mon, let's get busy. Jeremy, what are you doing?"

Hopping with glee, the trader waved a book at them. "This is an amazing place. I love it! Look, they even have a first edition of the *Choose Your Own Adventure* series. All this must be worth a fortune. I haven't seen stuff like this since I was a kid. It's wild!"

Eytan leaned toward Jackie and muttered, "Do you mind if I punch him?"

She frowned and clenched her fists. "Do you want me to hold him for you?"

An hour and one stern lecture for Jeremy later, they were all hard at work in what Eytan now called the Temple of the Imbeciles. While the two secret agents looked for a hiding place, Jeremy sat behind a counter, chewing on a pen and staring at the sheet of paper on which he had copied the numbers to the code on the back of the photo in the safe-deposit box. Crumpled pieces of paper were piling up next to the cash register. So far, all his columns, tables and grids had gotten him nowhere.

The meager light from the streetlights outside wasn't helping. Another fifteen minutes had passed when Jeremy shouted to the others, "Hey, smart-asses, stop everything. I've got it! My old man was so warped!"

"Or just paranoid, like anybody else who uses codes," Jackie replied. Exasperated by the time they had wasted, Eytan avoided making any caustic remarks. This was no time for jokes. Jeremy brandished a page full of figures and letters.

"Three first names. Jeremy, six letters. Daniel J., seven letters. Ann, three letters. And three lines with a series of numbers on them. After racking my brain, I used the keys provided by the names to decipher the strings of numbers and the four letters. In other words, six for the first line, seven for the second and three for the last. So with the Jeremy key, A, the first letter of the alphabet becomes seven, one plus six. Easy. Working from there, everything falls into place."

Eytan and Jackie stared at the trader with a whole new expression. This boy's mind was clearly made to do math. "So, what are we looking for?" asked the petite blonde.

"*La Chevauchée des Justes, Editions des Noirs Secrets, 1965.*"

"No kidding. We could have kept looking forever," Jackie muttered as she began to examine the spines of a row of books, looking for the title Jeremy had mentioned.

Eytan heaved a sigh of relief and pulled three copies of the novel from the highest shelf at the back of the store. No member of the public, except a giant or a guy with a ladder, could have gotten anywhere near the book. "Here it is. Three copies. Written by a guy named Thomel Gevoust. Never heard of him."

The yellow-tinged pages testified to the books' long shelf life. By opening each one to the last page, they soon found the edition they were looking for. They examined it from all sides, in vain. Eytan flicked through it, looking for another clue. In the end, he gave up, handed the book to Jeremy and leaned against a shelf, rubbing his neck. "We'll have to read the whole damn thing to find anything in there. Assuming there's something to find."

"You don't like to read, or you can't?" Jeremy teased, turning the pages.

"You're some comedian!" Eytan scowled, irritated.

"That's right," replied Jeremy, eyes riveted on the book. "But above all, I'm our resident code breaker, and I'm going to save us a whole stack of time again."

"How's that?"

"Because just by reading the chapter headings, I can see that from page one-twenty, what's printed in the book are my father's notes."

CHAPTER 32

September 8, 1985. A routine mission that turns into a fiasco isn't rare. But why reward the commanding officer of the mission instead of reprimanding him? The top brass have promoted me to lieutenant general and put me in charge of a department overseeing aircraft turnaround. Basically, I've been booted upstairs. Ever since, I can't stop wondering about what happened that day...

Opportunities to fly fighter planes were increasingly rare as my career progressed. But stars on your uniform are no replacement for the thrill of flying a mission. Quite the opposite.

So when the higher-ups asked me to pick three seasoned pilots for a test mission, I couldn't resist the temptation to put my name on the list. The F-16 was the jewel in the Air Force crown. For the occasion, it would be equipped with a revolutionary aiming system. Take-off would be from Fort Lauderdale...

After months of deadly dull bureaucratic routine and office politics, I grabbed the opportunity. Besides, being back in the frat house atmosphere of crews that couldn't salute me without making vulgar wisecracks would do me a world of good. I joined the military because I love my country. I stayed in it because I enjoyed the camaraderie of the Air Force. A shared passion for aviation creates strong bonds among characters with equally strong personalities. More than once, the rules were bent in order to do a risky maneuver or to get a one-up on other pilots. The brass turned a blind eye as long as no damage was done. If damage was done, though...

Even more than getting into the cockpit of the F-16, the flight plan got my juices flowing. After take-off, we'd be heading due south to take on an aircraft carrier and a group of mobile decoys before swinging back to base via the legendary Bermuda Triangle. That caused a lot of banter in the mess. Unstable weather conditions and, above all, pilot error could explain most of the so-called disappearances in the last fifty years. Even so, guys never failed to feel a twinge of excitement as they approached the zone.

On the big day, incredibly bad luck struck the mission. Lieutenants Jake Sokolove and Brian Stabbleford, fellow pilots and friends, were prevented from suiting up. Their physicals revealed that they both had heart conditions and therefore couldn't fly fighters. The medics even decided to keep them for observation. Military procedure, especially for top-secret Pentagon test flights, offers a host of options for the most unlikely scenarios, such as the last-minute grounding of two experienced pilots.

The spare wheels, as they are known, were called in. Richard Hoffman and Christopher Durham walked onto the tarmac. Both had just arrived from Edwards Air Force Base in the Mojave Desert, which had a reputation for spawning hotheads and daredevils. My cordial welcome soon turned into a full-blown Q&A session. I had to be sure my crew was prepared. Alongside other qualities, this thoroughness was a foundation stone of my career.

When I was satisfied, the pilots pulled on their helmets and climbed into their respective cockpits. I did likewise. The mission could begin. I applied full throttle but couldn't shake off an inexplicable sense of foreboding.

The operation went smoothly. I would even call it a total success, both in terms of the equipment we were testing and the crew's coordination. As tradition demands, Durham and Hoffman radioed me with their congratulations, and we headed back.

After a few minutes, we hit some clouds that didn't seem to present any danger. Suddenly, the other two planes dropped off my radar. I had no visual contact, and my attempts to radio them on every possible frequency met with no response. Suddenly, amid all the static, I picked up snatches of a conversation.

"They need to realize... BCI... lining its pockets." And "we... in the sun."

Those were the last words I heard Durham and Hoffman utter. The board of inquiry took barely three days to conclude that mechanical failure had led to the disappearance of the two planes and their pilots. I couldn't believe it. I knew my men. I didn't mention the conversation I overheard after the loss of visual and radio contact. Why? I don't know. Intuition, maybe. My transfer will be effective within one month. That gives me a little time to keep digging...

The checklists provided by the airbase maintenance crews never reached the Internal Affairs Division at the Pentagon. Nobody seems to know what happened to these important documents relative to the inquiry. An astonishing procedural snafu...

Durham's and Hoffman's files are untraceable on every computer at the base and on the Air Force's database. The people at pensions and benefits have no record of them. I called two friends at Vandenberg and Edwards. Nobody has ever heard of them...

I start my new job in seven days, two weeks earlier than planned. My investigation has annoyed the brass. I have to be more discreet and think of every possibility. Mechanical failure is a pretext to shelve the case. Two complete unknowns with phony IDs and mission papers have stolen two fighter planes. I'm sure of it. I have to find out what BCI means. But before that, I must get my hands on the records of incidents over the Bermuda Triangle. Sunday—tomorrow. Jeremy's sixth birthday. I'll work in the evening...

They're all fake! The disappearances over the Bermuda Triangle aren't at all mysterious. The legend is a smoke screen. I can't tell for sure about the civilian flights and the ships, but as for the military, and more specifically the Air Force, the data has been carefully massaged. I've dug up a confidential memo that mentions about twenty incidents involving the Air Force. An earlier draft of the same memo mentions no fewer than thirty-five disappearances, mostly bombers. I'm on the right track...

I'm Lieutenant General Corbin now. I should celebrate. I did with Ann and Jeremy yesterday. Ann is a rock. She knows I'm preoccupied, but she never mentions it. I have to watch myself. I'm not sleeping, and I'm on a short fuse...

Managing on-base personnel is my worst nightmare. I don't have a second to myself and rarely get home before ten in the evening. The last two months have been crazy, but not crazy enough to make me lose sight of my objective. Gradually, I'm piecing together the list of mysteriously vanishing aircraft and tracking down assignment details. But I sense the number of people I can call my friends is getting smaller and smaller...

An old friend called yesterday. We were at military academy together. Hearing from Bernard Dean was a real shot in the arm. He's going to drop by this weekend. I'll sound him out to see if he's picked up on the case. It could be useful to know someone with the CIA. But I'm walking on eggshells. I have to watch my step...

Ann and I hadn't seen Dean for years, and yet it felt like it was only yesterday. His charisma keeps growing, whereas I'm visibly withering. Constant stress and lack of sleep are mostly to blame. I never play with Jeremy anymore. I see no resentment in his eyes, just huge sadness. When all this is behind us, we'll get back to normal. Tonight, when Ann and Jeremy are asleep, Dean and I will have a little chat...

Dean didn't want to know. He advised me to be extremely careful for my sake and my family's. Basically, he told me to drop the investigation. But he'll be there if I get into big trouble. I sincerely hope it doesn't come to that, but it's not my style to let something like this go...

Without exception, the vanished bombers were all carrying enriched uranium. Besides the obvious danger of moving such sensitive materials by air, the transport of radioactive matter is by special permit only and strictly controlled. The military must, therefore, be involved in some kind of uranium-trafficking network, most likely linked to nuclear operations. So far, not completely surprising. National security transcends legal, administrative and even constitutional considerations. But when crews start disappearing, then we really are in murky waters...

A whole month and not a single new lead. The initials BCI correspond to no known military department. This whole business is becoming an obsession. I can't trust anyone on base. I've even started copying duty rosters to make sure nobody falsifies them. I have to get a grip. But I can't get one question out of my head: Where have the bombers, fighters and the damn uranium disappeared to?

I'm becoming irascible. Jeremy came home with a bad grade in math. I almost slapped him. That's not like me at all. I need to move on, or I'll lose my sanity and my family...

I was right! I couldn't put my hunch into words, but deep down I knew. I contacted Ed Jackson, a friend who works in the military's legal department. He told me he'd been investigating networks of traffickers in military secrets and radioactive material for years. He even works from a special office set up to bypass usual procedures and reduce the risk of leaks. The Soviets, Arabs and even the Chinese have all headed the list of suspects at one time or another, but nothing has ever been proved. I have dived headfirst into a big stinking mess. I've been ordered to drop it, but I know that it all has to do with those three letters. What can BCI possibly mean?

Ann and I had a big fight yesterday. I know she's worried, but she doesn't realize the importance of my investigation. She used Jeremy to make me feel guilty about never being home for him. I'll make amends when the time comes. Maybe I should get in touch with Dean. I know where to look.

Tomorrow, I head to D.C. for three days. The pretext is an air staff meeting to discuss the budget proposal going through Congress. We'll have to put up with the White House apparatchiks. I'm taking the whole file with me. Jackson said he'd meet me at the bar at the Watergate Hotel. He has a very questionable sense of humor...

The meeting never took place. I arrived late at the hotel, just in time to see paramedics carrying out Jackson's body. Heart attack. Surprising for a thirty-three-year-old athlete with no medical history. Before I slipped away, a waiter came over with a piece of paper Ed asked him to give to me just before he died. *The scribbled note contained just one word. A name, to be precise. Icarus...*

I'm making waves, rocking the boat. Requesting documents and asking questions wherever I go has attracted too much attention. Somebody's out to stop me and will use any means necessary. I have to be doubly careful...

Still no lead on BCI. It's infuriating. That's the key to the whole thing. I can sense it. I picked up the mail when I arrived home. In an envelope addressed to me, I found a bullet engraved with the word "Icarus." I think it's time to call Bernard Dean...

I'm trained for action. Tough decisions don't scare me. But nothing prepared me for the situation I'm in now. Bernard agrees with me. Whoever's calling me Icarus doesn't want me to get too close to the sun. My family's in danger. I've gone too far, but I can't turn back. Bernard offered to co-opt me into the CIA and put Ann and Jeremy under protection. He still wants nothing to do with my investigation, however. In the Secret Service, friendship has its limits. I'll be reunited with my family when all this madness is over...

I lay out the situation to Ann, frankly and honestly. She's a brave, strong woman. When she married me, she understood the nation's security couldn't be jeopardized, and I had an obligation. I feel her pain behind all the talk about me having to do my duty. Actually, it's about more than doing my duty to the country. I need to protect Ann and our son. He knows nothing. He wouldn't understand. He'll never understand. It's heartbreaking, but deep down, I'm convinced it's "see you later" and not "farewell..."

Two years. Two long years, gathering and crosschecking dozens and even hundreds of documents about missing consignments of uranium. In the United States alone, the volume is preposterous—over one hundred pounds. The floor of my sleazy studio-apartment hideout is carpeted with piles of paper. The walls are covered with sticky notes and sprawling charts. The only good news is that I've found a lead on BCI. There's a pharmaceutical company in South America with that name. I don't see how it ties in, but I have to explore even the slenderest leads...

I've traveled across Europe and Africa, pored over archives, visited embassies and consulates, met cultural attachés, the catchall word for our secret agents. Without any possible doubt, the network stealing radioactive material has a global reach. But I still have no lead on who controls it...

The collapse of the Soviet Republic is a blessing. The Berlin Wall fell less than six months ago, and already thousands of secret documents have emerged from the offices of the KGB. One document that that has reached us spells out the exchange of two U.S. Air Force planes equipped with experimental aiming systems in return for uranium. My planes. In the recipient box, no name, just a single word: Consortium...

1996. The Olympic Games are going to be held in Atlanta. While the world focuses on the athletes, I wander alone in a universe that scares me. A few weeks ago, I got a job working in the warehouse of a BCI subsidiary in Belgium. The company has expanded massively in the last twenty years to become a leader in its field. But the few records I got my hands on told me nothing new. I'm missing the key that unlocks the whole mystery, and I'm worried I'll never find it. These people know how to cover their tracks...

When I arrived at work this morning, a letter was waiting for me with an address in Zaventem, a suburb of Brussels. I'll pay a visit, but I have to be careful. My cover may be compromised...

I met an old man named Planic. He claims to have learned about my inquiries in the late eighties. He says he worked for the Consortium, and BCI is only a facet of it. He seems trustworthy. According to Planic, there's an organization deep in the corridors of power that's pulling the strings of history with terrifying cynicism and efficiency. Christ, these guys are nuts. I need to gather evidence to put a stop to them...

2001. The new millennium. I've lived in the same seedy hotel in a low-rent neighborhood in Paris ever since I left Brussels. Planic's revelations radically changed the course of my investigation. To understand the present and glimpse the future, I have to explore the past...

Years go by, and I become more and more decrepit. I glimpsed my reflection this morning while I was waiting for a bus to take me to a crucial meeting with an antiques dealer from London. Disheveled, bearded, bags under my eyes, moth-eaten coat—I looked like a bum. I'll have to get myself back in shape before I'm reunited with Ann and Jeremy. Tomorrow I fly to Florida to meet a specialist in objects that belonged to Nazi dignitaries. Without Planic, I'd never have stumbled across the SS lead...

My inquiries have left me in possession of a box and a key, priceless relics from the Second World War. The photo I found in the box sent shivers down my spine. Now all I need to do is put the finishing touches on my final report, the result of twenty-four years of stubborn research, discreet meetings, sleepless nights and constant glances over my shoulder. I'll give the most important pieces of evidence to Bernard for safekeeping until the federal government corroborates my conclusions and acts. Then I'll be able to be reunited with my family and get back to a normal life...

The walls of my studio rental in Paris are covered with press cuttings and archive documents. The Project is there, before my eyes. Danger is all around also. The woman in the bakery looks at me more and more strangely. Could she be one of them?

This morning, I ripped the wallpaper off my bedroom wall and drilled into it in places. The walls have ears. I'm sure of it. Day or night, I never drop my guard. Suspicious noises have convinced me that the demons are closing in on me...

I spend my nights in a cyber café and my days wandering the streets. I've outsmarted them. I've hidden my documents in a supermarket cart covered with cardboard boxes. Mumbling and grumbling, I push it along. People steer a wide berth around me. I've found the perfect cover.

Thanks to the Internet, I've been able to access the accounting spreadsheets that prove the Project's imminent implementation. Jeremy will be able to understand them. He has to!

I'm screwed. They've infiltrated my own government. They're everywhere. By making contact with my CIA liaison officer, I've signed my death warrant. I have absolutely no trust in this Pettygrow guy. He's working for them. It's obvious. My last chance to get the report into the right hands is Planic. Two people will have access to the documents that lead to this book. Bernard and Jeremy. If you're reading this, then I'm dead. I'm relying on you to finish what I started. Go to the address indicated in the contents and find Planic. He'll put you on the right track. Don't forget that the Consortium is an underground organization. To find it, you'll have to dig.

The notes ended there. The novel resumed in the next chapter. How Daniel incorporated his notes into the book mattered little. Jeremy stared at his father's last words. Cold, impersonal, reflecting the obsession that had overwhelmed him to the detriment of his family. He had hoped to find something else. A phrase, a mark of affection, anything that would reassure him of his absent father's love and convince him, however late in the day, that feelings always win out over national security.

What Jeremy held in his hands had a name. Insanity.

CHAPTER 33

Zaventem, Belgium, Saturday, 6:30 a.m.

The mind-numbing rows of sad redbrick houses remind me how much I like buildings that reach for the sky, textures, crowds you can blend into without fear. The city that never sleeps. Here, there are more cars than humans. The sidewalks are deserted. It reeks of boredom and suburban routine. Major companies apparently judge the area sufficiently alive to locate their R&D and logistical centers—even their head offices—here. And they say Manhattan is inhuman. If I could choose, I'd rather die anywhere that's not Zaventem!

For the last ninety minutes, we've been staking out, as the spies say, Planic's house. Eventually, the new day will dawn. Jackie's and my drawn features testify to complete exhaustion, but Eytan looks ready to compete in the Olympics. We watch the house windows, waiting for a sign of life. Finally, a light filters through the curtains in an upstairs window. Then another one downstairs.

Without a pause for thought, Buffy and the Jolly Green Giant leap out of the car, with me not far behind. Obviously. It's a long one-way street near a four-lane freeway and hotel for get-ahead executives. It's ugly. Which confirms my intuition that this place is a dump. On the other hand, it must be a great place to lie low.

The houses all look the same. Four windows upstairs, four downstairs, a vast front yard with perimeter fence. Plain, efficient and pukeworthy. I fire one up. The two spooks teamed up to stop me smoking in the car.

Eytan opens the gate and heads for the front door with Jackie right behind. I'm puffing away five yards behind. I miss New York. I miss Mom. Bernard, too. I'm tired. Jackie calls to me. I crush the butt underfoot. Eytan motions to me to move it. I speed up. A woman in her sixties opens the door, dressed to match the neighborhood. Black cardigan, gray blouse, dark pants.

"Can I help you?" she asks softly.

Let's leave this to Jackie. "We'd like to see Mr. Planic."

"And you are?" She scans our faces. Apparently dawn visitors are a novelty.

Eytan intervenes. "We're friends of Daniel Corbin."

The old lady asks us to wait and closes the door. Smart. For human interaction, a petite angel-faced blonde is better than a Golem over six feet tall. The Belgian Jane Doe appreciates good manners. And speaks good English. Not everything stinks around here.

Ten seconds later, the old lady reappears. The Belgian Jane Doe is a little too efficient for my taste. The others don't seem to share my suspicions. They're the specialists. We file straight into the living room. The house is opulently furnished in a style a retired British colonel would like. The kind of guy who collects random stuff on his travels to flaunt to his guests that he's seen the world. Bottom line, it's a tad overpowering. Three cracked brown leather Chesterfield sofas form a U around a teak Indonesian-style coffee table. The open northern hemisphere of a globe, held by a black statue of a naked woman with a prominent bust, reveals a well-stocked bar. It's undeniably tasteless. The walls are covered in still lifes with no real harmony of color or style. The ornately carved gold frames attest to a sickening snobbishness. Three corner tables laden with trinkets, ranging from Chinese statuettes to an antique clock, stand next to the three sofas. Two floor-to-ceiling windows at the back of the house offer a view of the wooded yard, hidden from the street. They're the only appealing aspect of this dark, sinister house. Lamps feebly illuminate the room in an ill-conceived attempt to provide a cozy atmosphere. Claustrophobia sufferers would hang themselves from the huge fan on the ceiling.

Eytan immediately sprawls on a couch and props his lumberjack boots on the table. Classy. I like it. Jackie frowns and whistles disapprovingly. Bald Eagle sighs and removes his feet. Jackie rolls her eyes. I'm surrounded by wackos. Nobody dares to utter a word that would shatter this house's religious silence, for fear of bringing bad luck.

A motorized hum comes from the stairs. I know that sound. A lift glides down a railing on the wall. Infomercials for these contraptions air all night long back home. The owner of the house must be disabled. Sitting on the gray metal seat, a man with parchment skin, a tuft of unruly white hair and tinted glasses slowly descends in the slender beam of light from upstairs. When it reaches the bottom, the lift motor cuts out, causing Pops to sway uncontrollably. He seems no longer human, but made of straw.

The old lady hurries down and fusses around this pale imitation of a man, releasing the straps that hold the seat in place. She presses a button on the back, and four wheels fold out. The ingenious device means people don't have to drag wheelchairs around the different floors of their home. The chair and its occupant take up a position at the far end of the table, facing us.

"Go make the bed, Annick. I'll call if I need you. Thank you." There's a surprise.

The moribund old fellow has the voice of a young man.

Annick impassively goes upstairs. The door clicks shut. When we are alone, Jackie speaks up. "Mr. Planic?"

"That's me. Please take a seat. If you'd like a drink, help yourself. Unfortunately, I can't do the honors myself."

He glances mournfully at his chair. He speaks excellent English, with just the hint of an accent. Slav, perhaps. I don't wish to jump to conclusions, but given his name...

Like two well-mannered children, Jackie and I sit side by side on a couch. God, she smells good. Eytan is the bad boy, sprawled defiantly on a couch all of his own.

"What brings you to my home?"

"We found this book in your bookstore. We're investigating…"

Before Jackie can finish, he interrupts, "You're investigating the death of Daniel J. Corbin. You found the book with his notes. At his request, I told my employee—I still own the store—to put the book on a shelf and never move it or sell it."

"Jeremy here is Lieutenant General Corbin's son. In his notes, Corbin mentions that you were a member of a secret society, which, as we have found out at a great cost of lives, has very sinister intentions."

Wow, she's smoking. Talking like a professor now. Beautiful, athletic, funny and smart. If I get out of this alive, I'll marry her. Or propose, at least.

"I broke off contact with the Consortium in 1995, when I moved here. The bookstore has been my cover for the last fifteen years. Every day, I expect to get a bullet in the brain. Every night, when I go to bed, I expect never to wake up. Yet I'm still here. I worked diligently for the organization for fifty years. My role was limited to keeping files on potential recruits. No more. At the time, my name was Andrei Kourilyenko."

As the old man tells his story, our jaws drop.

CHAPTER 34

"Your father came to see me a few weeks ago. He knew he was going to die. The Consortium's name for him was Icarus. Nobody before him had ever gotten so close to the truth. And like the courageous mythological Greek hero, he burned his wings. Daniel had unraveled the whole story. He held one end of the thread and couldn't help pulling it to see what he'd find. He soon realized that important government departments had been infiltrated. Anybody could be working for the organization. Some agents are never activated. Others are purposefully sacrificed. It's a cluster organization that is carefully compartmentalized to make those at its heart inaccessible. I call it a work of genius—sufficiently discreet to go unnoticed and powerful enough to influence the fate of humanity through its cunning maneuvers.

"Shortly after I was recruited by Bleiberg, at our first and only meeting, I began fastidiously researching the Consortium. It was impossible to put the chain of command down on paper, so I concentrated on an area that would arouse less suspicion, because it was the reason I had been hired—the recruitment of scientists, particularly those with an SS background. I also took the opportunity to expand my investigation into the history of the Nazi party."

Eytan interrupted. "Excuse me, but you said you met Professor Bleiberg in Berlin in 1945. He had been declared dead in the explosion that destroyed his research lab in 1942."

"Yet another maneuver to conceal his existence, Mr. ... Morg?" The Israeli agent frowned and nodded. "Please go on."

"In reality, the problem is knowing where to look. I got a lucky break when a particular incident came to my attention. The NSDAP received funds from various private sources, mostly businessmen. But there was an exception. Several million dollars had been channeled through a Spanish bank. Of all the documents I traced, only one mentioned that transfer. I crosschecked against Hitler's schedule of meetings and rallies. There was no obvious link to Spain, save for what I found in the visitors' book at Landsberg Prison, where Hitler was incarcerated after his failed putsch. The prison administration proved exceedingly lax with this particular prisoner but kept a complete record of his visitors. A name caught my attention. Adamet."

"Why that name?" asked Jeremy.

"It sounds Basque, doesn't it?" offered Eytan.

"Quite. It certainly stood out among all the Germanic names. Once more, after long and painstaking research, the lead took me to Adamet Epartxegui, the director of a regional bank in Bilbao from 1928 to 1936, when he left Spain to settle in Argentina."

Eytan racked his brain. The Argentinean tags on the car driven by Jeremy's attackers in Manhattan; A.E., the initials in Delmar's notes. Adamet Epartxegui. The pieces of the puzzle were falling into place.

"Why Argentina?" Jeremy looked like an enraptured student firing questions at the professor.

Eytan sighed loudly. "During the Spanish Civil War, a lot of Basques emigrated to the Americas. And they had strong historical links with Argentina. Now shut up and let the gentleman speak, OK?"

"I was just asking. How do you know all that?"

"Basque Country, ETA, terrorism, Mossad. Do you need me to spell it out?" Jeremy fell silent.

"Where was I? Oh yes. When he reached South America, Epartxegui simply vanished for eight years. He resurfaced in 1945 as the boss of a pharmaceutical company, Bleiberg Chemical Incorporated, which soon became BCI to keep the name Bleiberg off any official document. The capital came from all over—France, Japan, Britain, the United States. Millions of U.S. dollars, which was big money back then. The demand for drugs in the post-war years meant exponential growth and profits for the whole pharmaceutical industry. Governments all over the world placed orders with BCI. Soon the company was working with some very prestigious names. You've heard of them."

Eytan felt his stomach lurch. His voice felt like it was coming from outside his body, against his will. "Mengele, Eichmann, Kipp..."

"You might have to explain to your blank-faced friends." The old man's tone wavered between sarcasm and sincerity.

Eytan cleared his throat and stared at the floor. "After World War II, many high-ranking Nazis and their collaborators scattered around the world with the Allies' help, with the aim of countering Stalin's expansionism. Some settled in Austria, which bordered the Eastern bloc. Others emigrated to Latin America. Most didn't have to escape. They were helped by French, British and American secret services, which had a dual aim: funding dictatorships working for the CIA and exploiting the expertise these men had accumulated in various domains. The Nazis' war chest and scientific and industrial know-how bought immunity from prosecution and imprisonment for some of the vilest scum the world has ever known. Politicians call that pragmatism. The press talked about the scandal of former SS men living out luxurious retirements on the Rio de la Plata, but they hadn't retired. They were working for those countries' governments."

"The CIA did this?" Jackie asked, as if her world were crashing down around her ears.

"Don't be naïve. To counter communist revolutionaries in South America, the CIA supported a bunch of dictators. I know the Agency has done its best to erase what happened from the 1950s to the 1980s, but the facts are undeniable. The French were no better. A lot of wartime collaborators were included in a general amnesty and reinstated in the administration. Why? Pragmatism, of course. In a period of reconstruction, it's tempting to hold onto men with certain kinds of expertise without looking too closely at their pasts. That's the way the world works."

"But Mossad carried out several abductions of Nazis who were holed up in South America, didn't they?" asked Jackie.

For a moment, Eytan pictured himself as a history teacher dealing with an eager student. "Yes, with mixed results. Our biggest success was Eichmann's capture in 1960. Mengele always escaped us. We nearly cornered him, but he had support in high places and serious protection. Which reminds me, our opponents in the last few days struck me as a little wet behind the ears."

Eytan rubbed his thighs nervously. The old man spoke up. "You're right, Mr. Morg. The Consortium fails only when it decides to."

"We didn't beat anybody to get here, right? We just got rid of some people the organization judged expendable."

"Precisely. You catch on fast, Mr. Morg. Getting back to BCI, it's a major player on the stock markets through its subsidiaries and holdings in other multinational laboratories."

Jeremy jumped up, gesticulating madly. "I was right. I knew it! That's what the documents my father left us were all about. You know the turnover of the main players in the pharm industry? It's nuts. The top three in descending order: seventy-five billion dollars, forty-one billion dollars, thirty-five billion dollars. Whenever there's a health scare, they're suspected of bribing experts to ring the alarm bells and force politicians to launch crackpot vaccination campaigns. Remember the H1N1 virus? Nobody ever finds anything illegal, but stock prices go through the roof. The *London Times* article Eytan read to us mentioned lots of victims. So, this time, it's serious?"

"They are prepared to play with people's lives?" Jackie asked with disarming naivety. The other three stared at her wide-eyed. She winced. "I'll shut up."

Jeremy came to her rescue. "The answer is yes. Without hesitation, Jackie. But from what you said, Mr. Planic, it sounds like profits aren't this mysterious organization's only motivation. Am I wrong?"

"No. Money is the means to manipulate companies and politicians. But it's not the ultimate aim."

Jaw twitching, brows knitted, Eytan was losing patience. "Would you cut to the chase rather than keeping us in suspense? We'd all appreciate it."

"I understand your impatience, Mr. Morg. I'm an old man, and I have few opportunities to tell what I know. I just celebrated my ninety-third birthday. In other words, my life is over. I have greater respect for you, Mr. Morg, than you can ever know. For that reason, I will give you two vital pieces of information."

Eytan could hardly restrain himself. He sensed Jackie watching him, while Jeremy lapped up the old man's words.

"The Mexican epidemic will go global with alarming speed. People will die at a terrifying rate. Experts will panic, with good reason for once. Within a month, the whole planet will be gripped in terror. BCI will announce the discovery of an emergency vaccine. Given the colossal worldwide requirements, all the pharmaceutical companies will cooperate to produce and distribute it at a ridiculously low price because, apparently, the economies of scale are so massive. A few days later, vaccination centers and doctors will start giving jabs. Where do you think that will lead us, Mr. Morg?"

Eytan stood up, threw his head back and scanned the ceiling for a nonexistent horizon. His legs were shaking as never before. He wished he could crumple to the floor and let others solve the problems for him. He clasped his hands behind his neck.

"To the implementation of the Bleiberg Project on a planetary scale. But that's impossible."

"Which brings us to my second revelation. All the guinea pigs died of side effects from the experiments. Except one. The project's feasibility has been proved. Which is why it must be stopped. I tracked down the nerve center of the operation after your father's death, Mr. Corbin. You and your friends have the responsibility of bringing sixty years of history to a close. You must destroy the lab where the first stock of vaccines is kept. Rest assured, you won't have to go far. It's here, in Belgium."

§ § §

Andrei watched them walk away. He raged against the cruel weight of the years on his shoulders. They could act. He was condemned to wait in his damned chair for the end to come, feeling his faculties wane day by day. He summoned his nurse to wheel him back to the lift and recalled the day when Bleiberg, after informing him of the risks, offered him a shot of his magic formula. His fear of not surviving the treatment was too strong, and from that day on the shadow of death hung over him. Soon it would carry him off.

Stalin, then Hitler. Imperceptibly, the folly of men had worn him out, gnawed away at him. Fate had imposed on him a long, tiresome life and insidious decline. Wasn't that the reality of existence? In the end, the destination is always the same. Only the itinerary differs.

Annick tucked him into his bed and went back downstairs to prepare his morning coffee and toast and jam. Andrei let his gaze wander around the gray room. It was too big for a single man. Since his wife's death from cancer five years earlier, the life had gone out of his home. At least he still had the resources to pay for live-in care. He wouldn't end up in a hospice. Never mind if the old harpy lacked a sense of humor, she did her job diligently and with devotion.

In a few minutes, his inevitably lukewarm breakfast would arrive. Then he would engross himself in a book to pass the time until lunch. When nostalgia overwhelmed him, Dostoevsky's *The Gambler* was his only refuge. Alexei's dissolution would be his companion today. Reading in Russian reminded him of the motherland.

Annick was unusually slow today. First his visitors had revived painful memories, now they were delaying his daily regimen, which could interfere with his delicate digestion. The woman truly didn't understand the meaning of the word "fast." His ironic nickname for her was the Flying Belgian, which he thought was hilarious but didn't impress her. He called out and received no response. He gathered his strength and shouted louder. Panting, he heard slow footsteps on the stairs. He propped himself up on his pillows and folded the white sheets over his scrawny thighs.

"Good morning." It wasn't Annick's voice. It was younger, more resolute, devoid of emotion almost.

"Good morning, Elena."

"You don't seem surprised to see me."

"You have a lighter step than Annick, my dear. I fully expected to see you one day or another." He turned his head. You had to give the devil her due. She was magnificent. Tall, broad-shouldered, her athletic figure accentuated by tight jeans and long-sleeve top. What a shame that her face, once so gentle, had become so cold and sour. Her brown eyes, dark as the night, gave him gooseflesh. Her short dyed red hair accentuated her glacial beauty.

"You didn't hurt her, at least?" he asked with a tremor in his voice.

Elena walked around and stopped at the foot of the bed. "She didn't suffer, if that's what you want to know. Consider that a thank-you for accomplishing your final mission."

Another innocent life sacrificed to an absurd logic. Annick wasn't meant to die like that. "So, my turn has come. Wasn't one corpse enough? Why did you have to eliminate her?"

She smiled. "Have to? I wanted to. I don't like old folks. What does the great expert on the human soul have to say on the matter?"

He smiled back. "I say that you're mad, Elena. Look at you. Arrogant, haughty. You disgust me. I can't believe…"

Andrei's voice tailed off as a red stain splattered his pajama jacket. Behind the long muzzle of her revolver, Elena impassively watched the blood run down the old man's forehead and chest.

"You never believed. Otherwise you would never have betrayed our cause, Father."

CHAPTER 35

As soon as they were outside, Eytan ordered his two acolytes to get in the car. Before settling behind the wheel, he scanned the street without finding the slightest trace of a threat. He pulled away slowly. Jackie broke the silence. "This epidemic sends shivers down my spine. Eytan, how come Planic knew who you were?"

"The Consortium seems to be linked to many of my targets. It's hardly surprising they know me. We swim in the same murky waters."

"OK," cut in Jeremy, "but what's with this Bleiberg Project? I get the feeling you're holding out on us."

Staring at the road ahead, his shoulders hunched, the Israeli agent seemed to be carrying an invisible burden. "I didn't think the Bleiberg affair was directly relevant to the events of the last few days. Bleiberg was a pseudo scientist who experimented with genetic mutation for several years at the Stutthof concentration camp. As far as we know, he was never successful. I realize now that history has an annoying tendency to stutter."

"Perhaps. Now we have a slightly clearer idea of what this is about. I suggest we take a look at the facility Kourilyenko mentioned," Jeremy said eagerly.

"I agree," Jackie chimed in with the same enthusiasm.

Eytan let out a long whistle. "Sure. We go there, we eliminate everybody, and we take over the building before calling in the CIA and Mossad to close the place down. The only question left is which one of us will tour the TV studios telling the tale of our exploits?" He nodded and raised his eyebrows to reinforce his sarcasm.

"Why do I get the impression you're making fun of us?" Jackie asked, irritated.

"It's not just an impression. You're both raving mad. The BCI facility has to have security that's impossible to get past without being spotted, not to mention the patrols and guards. There are three of us. Our firepower is near nonexistent, and you two are both exhausted and inexperienced in missions of this scale. Going in there would be like entering the lion's den with a song and a dance. Forgive my reluctance to join you on your little escapade."

"So what's your wonderful plan, James Bond?" sniped Jeremy.

"I drop you at the airport, you catch the first flight home, and I take care of the rest. With a bit of luck, in a few days you'll see something in the papers about an industrial accident in the suburbs of Brussels."

Jackie picked up the torch Jeremy had lit. "Sorry to contradict your brilliant analysis, James, but I don't think we have a few days. The events of the last twenty-four hours demonstrate the Consortium's determination to mop everything up without delay. They know we have Corbin Senior's documents and that we're in Belgium, as shown by the attack at the rest stop. And a little bird tells me that a certain murderous bitch named Elena isn't too far away. Basically, if we don't act now, we give them time to make the contents of the facility vanish without trace."

Jackie's logic was irrefutable. Eytan felt like a snake was slithering up his spine to wrap itself around his throat. Anxiety took over his whole being. But his fear, whose bitter taste had been unfamiliar to him for so many years now, was not for his own safety. That's why he always worked alone. "You don't know what you're getting yourselves mixed up in. I'm talking about a short, targeted commando operation, not fighting off half-assed attacks like the ones you've faced since yesterday. This time, we're the attackers. You slip up, and that's it. It's over. We know nothing about the facility or its defenses, remember. We are ludicrously underequipped. Jackie can look after herself, and Jeremy, you've proved your bravery, but I'm not sure I can protect both of you in a situation like this."

Jackie and Jeremy shared a knowing glance and a wink. "Look, Eytan, forget about protecting us. Jackie knows her job, and I want to... no, I must finish what my father started. And if I find the bitch who killed my mother, I'll blow her away. I'm not a professional, I know. I'm better than that. I'm driven."

The stock trader's sincerity drew a smile from Eytan, which the others took to be a sign of approval. Many years of rubbing shoulders with danger and death around the world made the Mossad agent certain of one thing, but he kept it to himself. *The graveyards are full of driven amateurs.*

SOIGNES FOREST, *19* KILOMETERS SOUTH OF ZAVENTEM.

Fifteen minutes later, they were driving slowly past a natural barrier of tangled centuries-old oak trees and thick undergrowth and peering into the woods for a sign of the facility. The location seemed improbable, if not incongruous.

"Are you sure you entered the right coordinates from Planic into the GPS?" Jackie asked cautiously, expecting an angry response from Eytan. A series of heavy sighs confirmed her fears, and she went back to scanning the line of trees.

"You have to admit, it's a heck of a pretty forest," Jeremy muttered. "I'd no idea landscapes like this existed in Belgium. Near Brussels, too. Honestly, it's cool."

Jackie couldn't stifle a giggle. Eytan pulled into a rest area on the edge of the forest. He killed the engine and turned to his passengers. "I'll say this once. Cut it out. You're both beginning to get on my nerves."

Jeremy hung his head contritely. "Sorry, we haven't had much to laugh about in the last two days. Anyway, I guess you were right—no boots, no chainsaws, not even a Weedwacker. We are seriously underequipped!"

It was the joke that broke the camel's back. As the two of them killed themselves laughing, Eytan got out and stomped off, slamming the car door behind him. As he stood facing the forest, a smile flickered across his lips. On another day, he'd have found Jeremy's crack funny, but the thought of going back to squeeze the truth out of Planic/Kourilyenko didn't make him laugh one little bit. Trouble was, Eytan could have sworn the old man was on the level. His built-in lie detector had never failed him. Was it experience, instinct or an ear for the tiny inflections in a voice? He couldn't say. Whatever. He had expected to wind up in one of the many industrial parks around the Belgian capital. Instead, they were chugging aimlessly around a forest.

Car doors slamming informed him of the lovebirds' imminent arrival. Standing there with his hands in his pockets, the giant seemed perplexed. Jackie stepped to his right. Not seeing Jeremy, Eytan glanced to his left and saw the young man walking away from them. "Call of nature," Jackie muttered before Eytan could ask.

"I'm missing something," he said, hunkering down to stroke an adventurous fern poking from the undergrowth. "The old-timer wasn't lying. I'd bet my life on it."

"Me too," said the American agent. "I don't see why he would lie about this. By the way, can I ask you something?"

More questions about his motives, career or weapons. Get it over with. "Shoot."

"Do you think he likes me?"

Eytan straightened up and looked at her in bemusement. One was taking a leak, the other was regressing to high school level. With partners like them on a mission like this, maybe it was for the best that Kourilyenko had blindsided them.

§ § §

I can't hold out any longer. Exhaustion, I can handle. Guys trying to kill me, sure. But traveling always screws up my insides. That's why I leave New York only if absolutely necessary. Eight hours on a plane, seven in a car and liters of water downed since my fit in Zurich have thrown my bladder out of kilter. Vague notions of gallantry and, above all, the desire not to blow my chances with Jackie encourage me to urinate out of sight.

The morning's young, the road's empty. I savor the peace and quiet. The two superheroes will end up finding a way to send us to a certain death. I'm no soldier, and Eytan's right about our lack of firepower. I'm just glad I've played my part. Without me, their investigation wouldn't have gotten this far.

I walk past trees whose branches hang over the road and seem ready to devour anybody who ventures any closer to them. The four-lane highway cuts the woods in half. It looks like both sides are trying to merge and cover up the scar. Wow, either I'm turning into a poet, or I really am very tired.

I reach the perfect spot to find relief—a semicircular paved area separated from the road by a barrier of tires painted red, yellow and black, Belgium's colors. The barrier isn't to keep humans out, so I go in. It's a curious spot—too big to be a rest area—more like a parking lot with room for maybe twenty cars. Anyway, what the forestry engineers do with their country's natural areas is no concern of mine. But...

Taking a closer look to the left, I see a narrow overgrown trail. I bet it's an old lovers' lane. With my back to the road, I pee on a bush, whistling the *Sesame Street* theme so loudly and off-key that only an expert ear would recognize it. Strange how these moments of solitude lend themselves to creative thought. Scholarly studies show executives have their best ideas on the toilet or in the shower or bath. Not me. I zone out, gazing blissfully around me. Suddenly, my neurons switch on, my brain cranks into gear, and red lights start flashing.

Poking out of the branches of the tree above me is the muzzle of a rifle that's looking straight at me.

§ § §

The question had just slipped out. Jackie bit her lip, and Eytan even thought he heard her mumble a "you idiot" to herself. It was too late. Getting Eytan's opinion on her chances with Jeremy might have been her priority at that particular moment, but it was the last thing on Eytan's mind. Even so, his capacity to focus exclusively on his mission had reached its limits. Switching off until Jeremy got back wouldn't do any harm. And blowing her off wouldn't help matters. Maybe one good thing would come out of this whole damn mess. "Without a shadow of doubt, he likes you. Behind the cynicism, which makes even me laugh at times, a wounded but generous soul is hiding. Don't forget he carries heavy burdens. Even if he seems to be rediscovering his taste for life, he has a way to go before he resurfaces completely. Do you feel capable of helping him make that journey?"

"Capable, I don't know, but willing to try, I think. That's not a bad start, don't you think?"

Eytan smiled. "It's essential, I'd say. Say, the chump's been gone awhile. I'm not waiting for him to finish his pack to head back to Zaventem."

"You're right. It's been at least five minutes. Let's get him. A little walk will do us good." They headed off in the same direction as Jeremy.

"Say, are you single? A tall, handsome jock like you must have the ladies at his feet. No?" Eytan thrust his hands into his jacket pockets and hunched over slightly as he walked.

"Yes, I'm single. My missions leave no room for a private life. And yes, it appears that some ladies are not indifferent to my charm."

"You never found anyone you wanted to start a family with or just settle down?"

"I have no time to settle down, Jackie. And for a stack of reasons, I can't start a family." With a somber expression, Eytan began to stride out, forcing Jackie to trot every few paces to keep up with him. She fell silent. The awkward questions would have to wait. Eytan Morg was more comfortable talking about his profession than his private life.

In the woods and on the road, there was no sign of life. Jeremy had vanished.

The two agents reached a kind of semicircular parking lot carved out of the forest and separated from the road by stacks of used tires. In the middle, about fifty yards away, a body lay sprawled on the asphalt, arms outstretched.

Jackie started toward the body, but a powerful hand grabbed her arm and stopped her in her tracks. "Wait! Something's..."

Glancing at Eytan, Jackie saw a series of red dots dancing on his giant chest. "Kourilyenko didn't lie. We weren't looking in the right spot," she spat out.

Eytan stood motionless, like a wax doll. His powerlessness to react plunged him into profound despair.

"Listen, Jackie, and never forget: Never surprised, always alive!"

Blood splattered the young woman's face. She jerked her head away as the Israeli agent went down.

CHAPTER 36

Lightweights! We walked into the trap like a bunch of beginners. Great job, guys. Out for a stroll with our hands in our pockets, not even realizing we were in the right place. I have an excuse, but Buffy and the Jolly Green Giant? Amazing!

The Consortium boxed cleverly, I suppose. Building an underground facility on the site of an abandoned racecourse in the forest, now that's industrial genius. Protected by nature, they can work undisturbed. The crumbling buildings above ground house advanced surveillance systems. The staff entrances are hidden under the old racecourse stands, and deliveries are made via a ramp that opens in the grass in the middle of the track. It's not a racecourse anymore; it's a Swiss cheese. The basement is a tangle of pistons and giant pumps. God knows how much it cost to build all this. A fortune. It's crazy. They built a factory under the forest. Wacko! And like the moron I am, I've chosen one of the many parking lots nearby to take a leak. If we'd just gone an extra thirty yards, we'd have found it.

I recall my father's words: *The Consortium is an underground organization. You'll have to dig.* Now we know where I get my warped sense of humor.

Four muscular guards shove us toward a steel door. This hallway is never-ending. With the constant turns, the place is a real labyrinth. It's the epitome of a Hollywood secret army base—gray concrete walls, rows of fluorescent lights, painted markings on the floor (comprehensible only to qualified personnel) and the building names: B23, C5 and so on. The nerve center of a celluloid conspiracy. But Eytan's wound confirms that their guns don't fire blanks. I'm amazed he's still standing with a slug in his shoulder. He shows no pain, not even a tiny grimace. At the very most, he's a fraction paler than usual.

Flanked by two gorillas, Jackie looks tiny. Even I feel small surrounded by these hulking brutes. Jackie glances anxiously at me. I give her a wink. She smiles slyly back at me. Buffy has a plan. I'd bet my life on it.

The bitch walks alongside me. She's impressive. Beautiful. One of those cold, distant beauties whose eyes burn into your soul but stop you from getting the tiniest glimpse of her heart. Compared to Jackie's soft, curvy features, Elena's face is harsh and angular. She stares haughtily at me with her brown eyes. I stare right back, enjoying her disdainful gaze, wondering what she'll look like when I break her neck.

Our forced march ends abruptly outside a reinforced door. Elena swipes a card across a scanner in the wall. Noiselessly, the doors slide into the walls. It's pitch dark. Impossible to see a yard in front of your face. As if the room into which the guards push us could absorb any light. Judging by Eytan's expression, it could also suck up all hope. But I remain convinced that with Jackie's help he will turn the situation around. Or maybe I'm just fooling myself.

The door closes behind us. The lights don't just come on; they explode in a blinding flash. We shield our eyes until we get used to them. The guy who designed this place was a psycho. Clinically insane. We're in a huge space. A truck would get an inferiority complex in here. On the side walls, green liquid bubbles in tanks that are ten feet high and six feet wide. They're flanked on each side by three cylinders connected to supply tubes that lead to a utility duct in the ceiling. Even scarier are the adjacent hospital beds with white sheets, patient charts and monitoring units, like those Mom was hooked up to more than once. EKG machines, a pump and a brain-function gadget. The sight of that here gives me a nasty sense of foreboding. Just like the yellow radiation signs everywhere.

Some math a day keeps the panic away. Three tubes multiplied by two sides. That makes six tubes, so six beds. The only question is, why is that goon booting up three monitoring units?

Jackie, Eytan and yours truly. OK, I can panic now.

§ § §

Eytan's shoulder was causing him agony. The small-caliber bullet had lodged in the flesh without fracturing the bone, but the bleeding wouldn't stop. Their opponents numbered four, plus the tall redhead. Not a huge problem in normal circumstances. But with only one arm and his hands cuffed, the situation didn't look good. Jeremy was showing all the clinical signs of fear. Sweat dripped from his forehead. His breathing was shallow, and his eyes were bulging. Eytan couldn't blame him. It was impossible to swap a trader's lifestyle for that of a hit man, for whom danger, if not a daily companion, was a regular acquaintance. Unfortunately, Jeremy seemed destined to become a collateral victim of these secret wars, just as the young Polish Jew had become the victim of a hate-fueled dictator he never actually saw. Eytan couldn't bring himself to give up. Not now.

Not after so many years of struggle and sacrifice. And definitely not without a fight.

He quickly scanned the room and made a mental note of the order in which his enemies would die. His concentration was broken when the main door opened, and a man in a white coat entered, hands clasped over his chest, fingers intertwined. Anywhere else, it might look as if he were praying. He wore the kind smile of a grandfather welcoming his grandchildren for Christmas. Short gray hair framed a broad forehead over small, alert eyes.

"My friends, what a pleasure to see you all here! Your father was a real thorn in our side, Mr. Corbin. If only you knew. As for you, Ms. Walls, I learned of your existence only yesterday, but according to Elena, you have acquitted yourself well. I'm not forgetting that legend of the Israeli secret services, the one and only Eytan Morg. I'm honored!"

First, the Hollywood set. Now, the mad scientist. Jeremy swiftly interrupted. "And who are you?"

"How forgetful of me. Of course, how could you know? You could figure it out, I suppose, if nature had given you a more highly developed intellect. Despite your ignorance, you would make an acceptable laboratory rat." Jeremy stared narrowly at the man.

His head down and his eyes shut, Eytan answered the question. "Bleiberg."

The professor smiled. "You don't know the whole story, do you? At the most, you have a few scraps of information on which you have founded hypotheses that your limited minds refuse to accept. Granted, you are missing some fundamental facts. I can't resist the temptation to give you a more ample explanation. It's a common weakness among unrecognized geniuses. Let's take a brief journey into the past, shall we?

"The Nazis were desperate to prove the superiority of the Aryan race. Their dogma drove them to investigate every possibility, even the most hare-brained. Whole expeditions were wiped out looking for non-existent mystical artifacts and submerged continents. But the truth lay in science. The Nazis' extremism led the Consortium to facilitate Hitler's rise to power and encourage his thirst for conquest. I see a question in your eyes. Why? The answer is perfectly simple. We believe in human evolution through science, thought and logic. Our aim is the creation of an intellectual and physical elite. But it's a complicated quest, requiring enlightened minds and brains, visionaries, colossal resources and, above all, moral adaptability. By creating the Third Reich, plunging the world into war and ordering the extermination of the Jews, Hitler and his clique created the conditions for technological advances unprecedented in human history. The arms race led to the invention of radar, new propulsion techniques and new industrial norms. Must I remind you how much the conquest of space owes to German scientists who joined NASA?

"I was a young researcher when the Consortium recruited me in 1941. It was a godsend. I had no doubt as to the fate the SS reserved for me because of my Jewish origins. The deal was simple. The Nazis already had adequate facilities, test subjects, raw materials and a competent research team. In return, they would never have access to my discoveries. Most amusingly, the organization was informed of my research through Rudolf Hess. In fact, it was thanks to his disastrous expedition to Scotland that I came to their attention. But what research are we talking about? Genetic mutation, of course. The acceleration of human evolution. That was my project. The *Übermensch* is not a myth. The body possesses untapped potential. It merely requires awakening. That's where I come in. The injection of a radioactive solution provokes a modification of the genome with striking results: a drastic slowdown of the aging process, an increase in lung capacity, an improvement of neurotransmission and other beneficial changes that you are not capable of understanding.

"Naturally, the first trials were failures. The injections killed the subjects instantly. Gradually, I obtained longer survival periods, but the subjects developed cancerous tumors. Success arrived after three hundred and one failures. Subject 302, a Jewish child from Warsaw, survived the treatment. I had perfected a serum that blocked the cell necrosis that caused cancer. The child would be dependent on it all his life, but at least my theories had been shown to work. In time, further development of the formula would completely eliminate cell necrosis. In 1942, two weeks after the end of the protocol, Heinrich Himmler visited my facility at the hospital in the Stutthof concentration camp in Poland. I couldn't allow Subject 302 to fall into the hands of the Nazis. The Consortium would have made me pay dearly. Furthermore, my research team was no longer of any use to me. I therefore organized the complete destruction of my laboratory. Only my notes, my guinea pig and I were to survive. A tunnel would take us to a truck driven by my contact in the Consortium.

"Unfortunately, the situation got out of hand. Perhaps as an unexpected side effect, the child's intelligence developed exponentially. He activated the explosives early. Himmler survived, as did I, miraculously, but my masterpiece escaped in the confusion with the only existing doses of the serum and, annoyingly, the formula."

"You're totally insane," shouted Jeremy. "You seriously expect us to buy your superman story?"

The corners of Bleiberg's mouth creased as his lips twisted into a stiff smile. Eytan felt as if his heart had stopped. "My poor boy, you doubt that I am telling the truth?"

"Got it, egghead!"

"You seem very forthright, Mr. Corbin. What would you say if I told you that Subject 302 is in this very room?"

CHAPTER 37

A VILLAGE NORTH OF WARSAW, OCTOBER, 1940.

The children ran through the long grass in the field alongside the region's solitary road. Roman was so small, his head appeared only when a gust of wind buffeted the grass. As usual, an eager smile was etched on his face despite his missing teeth. The smile got wider as he came closer to catching his brother, who was not only bigger and faster, but also smart enough not to dishearten Roman. They could keep playing this game indefinitely, but Old Bartocz would tan their hides if he caught them gamboling around on his small property.

The chase continued until Roman's asthma sapped his energy. The attacks were increasingly frequent. The boys were allowed to play outside only if they promised to be especially careful. The chase always ended by the old tree. With the agility of monkeys, they climbed to the biggest branches, from which they would while away the afternoon contemplating the scenery.

Today was no exception. At the foot of the thick gnarled trunk, Roman gasped for breath, but his hands knew every hold. He swiftly reached the branch from which his brother would haul him up next to him.

Sitting side by side, they sparred and punched each other on the shoulder. "Three times three?" demanded the older brother.

"Three times three equals three threes," said the younger brother. They laughed.

"No, three times three is six."

The answer was accompanied by another playful punch. Roman answered a dozen more simple questions without fooling around. In their family, education was no laughing matter. Their father, the local doctor, emphasized the need to learn and, above all, understand. "It's the only way to control of your destiny," he never tired of telling them. "Knowledge unlocks every door for you if you use it right."

With the encouragement of their mother, the children integrated learning into their play. With their lessons finished, they settled down to watch the day decline. The sound of an engine drew their attention. Trucks were a rare sight in the region, and cars even rarer. They peered down the road usually traveled by horse-drawn carts. A long column of vehicles bristling with men in uniform stretched as far as the eye could see. In the lush landscape, the gray cohort seemed to tear the world apart.

"Roman, we have to go home. Now!" Dumbstruck by a spectacle he didn't understand, the little boy didn't say a word. As fast as Roman's asthma would allow, they ran back to the village hand-in-hand.

By evening, an overwhelming number of German troops were occupying the small town, whose populace made no attempt to resist. Indeed, here and there, a few inhabitants welcomed them with cheers. Grouped together and surrounded by a dozen guards with machine guns, the children watched incredulously as a strange spectacle that was beyond their comprehension took place.

The men of the village were lined up in a row facing soldiers who stood stiffer than old Bartocz's fence posts. A peasant farmer walked by, his cap pulled down over his ears and a handkerchief clutched to his mouth, so only his eyes were visible. He stopped and pointed an accusing finger. "Him! The doctor. He's Jewish."

An hour later, when the sun finally dipped behind the hills, father, mother and sons emerged from their house in the square opposite the village hall with suitcases in hand.

The older brother, who hadn't spoken for hours, shuffled closer to his parents. "Dad, it was Ignaziewski who denounced you. I recognized him, even though he was covering his face. Why'd he do that?"

The father ruffled his son's curly brown locks. The child's maturity filled him with pride and joy. Roman was following in his brother's footsteps. Two fine boys. "You're right. It was Ignaziewski. I recognized him, too. People sometimes do incomprehensible things out of fear. Or hatred."

"But you cured his flu last winter."

"True. But that was last winter. Things have changed. The world has changed."

"I thought he was your friend."

"I thought so, too. It's human nature, Eytan. Human nature."

§ § §

The march was long and painful. For three long days, Yitzhak, Alina, Roman and Eytan Morgenstern trudged forward, flanked by armed vehicles and men. They stopped in every village, every tiny hamlet, to play out the same unchanging pantomime. They were joined by one family, then ten, then a hundred. The new arrivals' protests soon gave way to silence and despair. The Germans showed no leniency, no compassion. Dissolved in this human tide, they finally reached Warsaw. Few of the local population dared even glance at the marchers. The soldiers had the city in a stranglehold, stifling every sign of life.

The column—herd, Eytan thought to himself—stopped. Only the sobbing of children could be heard above the rumbling tanks and deafening, repetitive thump of boots on cobblestones.

German officers designated leaders and informed them of the rules in the area where the Jews were to be consigned. The news spread rapidly through the marchers' ranks. Some clung to the hope that this forced reorganization of their lives was only temporary. The situation wasn't good, but it was bearable.

§ § §

The following days and weeks removed any doubt as to the German occupiers' intentions toward the Jewish community. From a few hundred, the population of the small area rose to a few thousand and eventually reached three hundred thousand people.

At gunpoint, the Jews were forced to put up a perimeter wall, building their prison within the city. The streets filled with a motionless crowd, bystanders of their own tragedy. Sitting on sidewalks, old folks bartered mementoes of a life of hard work for cigarettes and food. Filth took over, as scarce water supplies made basic hygiene impossible. Cramped living conditions didn't help matters. In the Morgenstern's apartment, twenty people eked out an existence in a space intended for four. The family didn't complain. The last to arrive were packed into damp cellars overrun by rats and vermin. Infections proliferated, and disease was rampant.

The guards of their pestilential prison provided nothing except one meal a day. And what a meal! Thin gruel and a slice of stale bread. Absolutely insufficient for the old folks and children huddled around cold, desperately empty pots. Malnutrition ravaged the inhabitants. A typhoid epidemic spread terrifyingly fast.

Despite frequent, brutal raids orchestrated by the Germans, Yitzhak Morgenstern and other doctors set up makeshift infirmaries in the least putrid cellars. Illegal schools bloomed in apartments that were deserted during the day. Education had become a crime. The death of the mind preceded that of the body.

The grown-ups' defiance and determination to maintain the shaky façade of normal life inspired the children to make their own small contribution. A small group led by Eytan loosened bricks in the northern section of the wall. Ingeniously, they opened up a tiny passage to the outside world. No adult could get through. But it enabled them to orchestrate a nightly plunder of bread and vegetables.

Roman had just celebrated his sixth birthday. He was losing strength, because the foul air aggravated his asthma, but he was as cheerful as ever and followed his brother everywhere, except when Eytan led his brigade, as he called it, on a raid into the city. That evening, the little boy pleaded with his older brother to take him with them. "Simon's only six," he argued reproachfully. "And you let him come."

"It's too dangerous, Roman. You have to run fast without stopping. It's not an old farmer who'll be chasing us if we're spotted. Stay here and keep watch. If nobody notices you, you'll have won a point, OK?"

Sulking, the little boy hunkered down to keep lookout from the protective shadow of an electricity pole while the gang got to work removing the red bricks from the wall.

Fog inexorably wreathed the sleeping ghetto like a ghost, infiltrating every nook and cranny and protecting the boys in their perilous but heroic undertaking. The Germans' unbending discipline had its advantages. The arrival of their patrols could be predicted to the nearest minute. They were machines. Their punctuality delighted Eytan, whose watch had been confiscated, along with the meager goods the family had been allowed to bring with them. He had learned to keep perfect time in his head.

A few apples and some warm bread, furtively passed through a gap in the window by a sympathetic old lady, were the expedition's only spoils. They had only a few minutes left to get back into their open-air prison. A gentle but glacial breeze blew through Warsaw.

The children flitted down the street like shadows on the walls of the building at the street corner opposite the ghetto. One by one, they made the frantic thirty-yard sprint to the tiny gap in the wall. As always, Eytan was last to go.

On all fours, peeking through the hole, Roman waited for his brother while the others grabbed the bricks, ready to cover their tracks as fast as possible.

The breeze picked up, and harsh gusts of wind blew through the rundown streets and avenues of the occupied city, brutally dispersing the fog. As he ran, Eytan dropped three apples, which bounced off the sidewalk and scattered on the cobbled road. He scrambled to pick up the precious food whose curative properties his father constantly praised.

Roman peered up and down the street. The distinctive sound of boots on pavement warned of the soldiers' imminent arrival long before the patrol came into sight. Then, behind Eytan, four soldiers smoking cigarettes emerged from the mist, rifles over their shoulders. Two of them held German shepherds on leashes. For fear of giving away the location of the hidden passage, Roman didn't cry out. Instead, without hesitation, he ran toward his brother who was still ten yards from safety, gathering the last apple.

Cursing his clumsiness, Eytan looked up and immediately recognized his brother's frail silhouette and awkward running style. A gunshot rang out. Roman kept running. A second gunshot covered the dying echo of the first. The little boy crumpled face-first on the ground.

Despite the barking dogs and screamed orders, Eytan rushed to him. Tenderly, he raised the little head, placed it on his lap and brushed aside the curly brown locks. Those closed eyes would never open again. Pain seared Eytan's stomach. He opened his mouth and waited for a cry that never came.

A rifle butt sent him flying. On his side, dazed, Eytan saw a boot slam twice into Roman's corpse. He would join his brother in a few seconds. Death would be a release.

The patrol's commanding officer hesitated before giving the order to shoot. Two machine guns pointed at the boys like snakes seeking the best angle of attack. Finally, a decision was made. Solid hands grasped the child. He was hauled away through the dark streets, intermittently illuminated by shapeless, dirty haloes of light from the tall street lamps. Through blurred eyes, Eytan saw the tailgate of a green truck identical to those he and Roman had seen arriving in their village a handful of months earlier, when life still had meaning. Around the vehicle, spotlights shot through the darkness. Forlorn rolls of barbed wire protected it from a nonexistent revolt. He was thrown aboard like a bale of straw loaded on a farmer's flatbed. He rolled across the metallic grooves in the floor of the truck, surrounded by motionless men and women—silent, petrified, waxwork figures.

Four soldiers climbed up, and the truck juddered away. The elder Morgenstern boy slumped into welcome unconsciousness, leaving behind him the insane and evil grown-ups' world.

§ § §

But that merciless world, devoid of affection, devoid of the slightest trace of love, revived him. Eytan was shaken around like a rag doll. He opened his eyes and winced in the dazzling light aimed at the back of the truck, from which a guard expelled him with a series of kicks. He nearly fell on the rocky ground, but his agility kept him upright and provoked sarcastic whistles of admiration from the soldiers gathered around the tailgate.

The sight before the boy's eyes wrenched his gut. He watched helplessly, with no chance of comprehending, as men, women and children were unloaded like livestock from trains and lined up facing the guns of cold, expressionless soldiers. The jagged outline of tall chimneys scarred the sky, pumping out nauseating smoke. The landscape of posts, barbed wire and barrack huts was an ode to hatred and destruction. The barked orders of the guards drowned out the silent sobs of a tortured people.

Eytan expected to join the cohort of prisoners, but a German grabbed his arm and dragged him over to a group of three men in white coats, who were chatting and even swapping jokes as they smoked their cigarettes. The soldier's heels clicked together, and he launched into an incomprehensible explanation. One of the doctors—whose stethoscopes convinced Eytan of their function—nodded toward a small stone building nearby. Eytan was whisked away. Inside the building, as he sat on a stool, his head was shaved, and a number was tattooed on his forearm. The pain was nothing, compared with the humiliation. Torn from his parents, separated from his little brother, deprived of the freedom he loved, he was now stripped of his identity, his status as a child and, worst of all, his humanity. Treated like an animal, he refused to give his persecutors the satisfaction of seeing him cry or struggle in vain and took refuge behind a wall of silence, withdrawing deep into himself.

The man in the white coat examined him thoroughly, tested his reflexes, took measurements and carefully noted everything on a brown card that he pinned to the boy's sweater.

Ten minutes later, Eytan was escorted across the railroad tracks and loaded into a curious train composed of a locomotive and single car. Inside, about twenty children gazed at the new arrival. Most were huddled against the wooden sides of the car. A few were in tears. As soon as Eytan was aboard, the heavy door slid shut.

A long, painful journey began. Yet another.

The last one.

§ § §

The children sought a sign of affection, a hint of love, in the eyes watching them, but Eytan soon realized that love had been banished from this place. In turn, he banished the questions that assailed his mind. How? Why? The answers were no use to him. Their existence was no longer their own. An animal intended for the slaughterhouse received more consideration. Understanding was impossible. Like the reasons for the second tattoo, whose brutal and painful application resulted in fearful beatings for those who cried. All for three extra numbers! Eytan tugged at the sleeve of his sweater and knotted it with his handkerchief, the only possession that the guards, reluctant to handle snotty-nosed kids, had deigned to leave him.

The new camp offered them the sight of more barbed wire, watchtowers and endless rows of wooden barracks. The first snows were beginning to stick. The sun shone and reflected on the immaculate white expanse but brought no warmth. Seeing the building toward which they were being herded, one of the kids screamed for joy. After all, aren't doctors kind and considerate? And the man at the top of the steps staring at them, arms crossed, who could he be if not a doctor?

The child's only reward for his show of enthusiasm was a smack on the back of the head so violent that it propelled him face-first into the snow. In German, the doctor sternly rebuked the guard, who sheepishly fell back, while the medic hurried down the steps to the boy. He carefully turned him over and examined him, without returning the child's smile. They both stood up. The man's dark eyes locked onto Eytan's hostile glare. A wink and a sentence in Polish. A single sentence that defined a whole life. "I don't want any damage to come to my rats." Eytan clenched his fists hard enough to break his knuckles. That's what they were to him. Rats.

As they were marched into the building that was a hospital in name only, Eytan passed by the doctor, who had returned to his position at the door. With no regard for the possible punishment, including death, he announced in the calmest, coldest voice possible, "Some rats bite."

The man in the white coat smiled, then closed the doors of a place that adults called hell.

CHAPTER 38

I'm floundering in a lunatic asylum. They're all absolutely out of their minds, but Pops takes the cake. I'm going to be murdered by a bunch of maniacs. We all go through tough times, but I'm breaking all records in the life's-a-bitch category. "Cut out the Subject 302 bullshit. It's ridiculous. If you were Bleiberg, you'd be ninety-five years old at the very least. You barely look older than sixty. I'm not buying your half-assed story."

"My formula stops the aging process. In the case of a subject who is still growing, the process stops around the age of twenty-eight, at the peak of his or her physical development. The subject will suffer no loss of faculties over time until natural death occurs around the age of one hundred or one hundred and twenty, according to my calculations. However, if the subject is already over thirty, the aging process is frozen at the time of the injection. Amazing, don't you agree?"

"You nutcase!" I feel such pure hate for this guy, the insults are going to get a lot worse if he keeps this up. Pops comes over. One more step, and we're in making-out range. He whispers, "Do you know that the dermatologist Daniel Cornelius Danielssen made several attempts to contract leprosy to prove it was infectious? Do you think I hesitated for a moment before injecting myself with the mutagen? That is the cost of scientific progress. Now imagine a human being whose movements are so swift and precise, they're imperceptible to the naked eye. You can never beat that kind of agility and speed. This human's reaction adapts to the requirements of any given situation. Imagine a human who never loses control of his emotions, who always makes the right decision at the right time. Does that not remind you of someone?"

I glance at Eytan. Bleiberg approaches the giant. He grabs his right arm and roughly tugs the blood-stained sleeve of his shirt up to his elbow. Eytan winces in pain but doesn't cry out. A letter and six figures are tattooed on his forearm.

"Allow me to introduce Eytan Morgenstern, a Polish Jew who at the age of eight the Nazis sent to the new camp at Auschwitz. Selected by the guards who used medical criteria defined by my team, he was transferred to Stutthof, my research facility, to become..."

Bleiberg lets go, takes one step sideways and repeats his demonstration with Eytan's left arm. This time, the tattoo consists of three figures. Three, zero, two.

"... Subject 302. My first masterpiece."

Eytan lowers his head toward the old man. His face is a portrait of infinite contempt. "By claiming it's a vaccine, you're going to inject the whole planet with your shit, aren't you? Money doesn't interest you. So why? And why now?" Eytan doesn't speak the words, he spits them out.

"If only you knew how wonderfully proud you make me. I've been following your exploits for years. Ever since your mission with the commando unit assigned to abduct Eichmann in 1960. How old were you then? Twenty-seven? It's amazing. A half-century later, and you don't look a day older. Look at what awaits you, my dear." Bleiberg cups Jackie's cheek with one wrinkled hand. She stares at him in disgust. It looks like she's fighting the urge to spit in his face.

He comes back over to me, looking smugger than ever. "To satisfy the fantasies of Himmler and his clique, my first experiment incorporated minor subsidiary mutations, such as increased growth and, in Eytan's case, a modification of hair color. I turned his brown hair blond. Even as a child, he couldn't stand it. Something tells me that he didn't grow used to it as he got older."

He glances at Eytan. "How long do you spend shaving your head and face every day?"

No answer. The giant's silence pains me. I never thought I'd see him so distraught that he couldn't speak. Eytan Morg knew more about the Bleiberg Project than he was letting on. He was the Bleiberg Project. But how could you blame him for keeping silent about this monstrosity? Anyway, are there words strong enough to describe the inconceivable?

I'm sick of this. "Shoot us and get this over with. If it weren't for your gorillas, you shriveled little shit, I'd beat you to a pulp."

"I don't want to kill you, Mr. Corbin. Perhaps not, at least. And this will answer your question, Eytan. The mutagen has a life of its own. Each organism reacts differently. We had to carry out tests on a massive scale. A handful of enlightened dictators around the world allowed me to work in total secrecy on political prisoners. I am now able to say that thirty percent of the subjects survive the treatment. The rest die within two minutes, three for the most resilient. Science will decide your fate, not I."

Put a bullet between our eyes, dammit! For pity's sake, I don't want to wind up a guinea pig for a modern-day Frankenstein.

"As for why the operation is taking place now, there are two answers. First, it took me fifty years of hard work under the radar to develop a serum that could be produced in industrial quantities. Second, seven billion humans now sully the planet. Nine billion by 2050. Before the end of the year, we will reduce that to two or three billion at the most. Humanity will have taken a crucial step in its evolution. The survivors will form one single race. Unemployment and poverty will be eradicated. Nutrition and environmental issues will be solved in one fell swoop. What can I say, Mr. Corbin? I'm an incurable ecologist."

He's not even joking. The guy totally believes what he's saying. Billions of innocents will die to satisfy the megalomania of a madman.

"Now, if you don't mind, I'll move onto my final experiment with my favorite guinea pig," Bleiberg says, turning to his guards. "Show them into the waiting room."

Seeing the evil smiles of the four assholes, I fear the worst.

Before she is ushered out, followed by two chaperones, Jackie raises her hands in the air and yells to Eytan, "2003!" She gets a whack in the back for her trouble but ignores it.

2003. Fat lot of good that does us.

§ § §

The two men shoved Eytan toward a bed.

"My child, I assume you haven't forgotten the pain that is inherent to the mutation process. You are going to help me once more in my research. I've no idea what might happen when the mutagen is injected into a subject treated with my original formula. Thanks to you, I'm going to find out."

The so-called doctor took a plastic-wrapped syringe out of his white coat and headed toward the beds. Eytan struggled to break free. His head was buzzing. Panic was clouding his brain. Not this. Not again. He recalled the incessant jabs, the ensuing convulsions, the debilitating pain. And the fear that filled his cell with every new day that dawned.

One day, he was so terrified he wet himself. Beside himself with anger, Bleiberg had him hosed down to teach him good manners. The SS guards laughed at the naked child as he clumsily tried to protect himself from the icy water. Then they dragged him into the laboratory by his arms, hammering his back every time he screamed. Eytan learned very young that crying out offers no protection. That morning, on Heinrich Himmler's orders, an official in a black uniform came to take pictures of the doctor and his guinea pig. At the precise moment the flashbulb popped, facing these soulless, compassionless, loveless monsters, Eytan discovered the power of his anger.

One way or another, sooner or later, without a second glance, without remorse, he would kill them all.

§ § §

I don't dare to imagine what the waiting room looks like. Two clowns lead us down the drab, empty hallways of the complex. It's Saturday morning, and apparently even the bad guys give their staff the weekend off.

Jackie looks astonishingly laid back. I've no idea what she's got in mind, but I'd welcome any initiative with the great pleasure. We've reached the waiting room and, judging by the symbol on the gray double doors, it doubles as the crusher.

A card is swiped across a scanner, and the room opens up to us. The doors are not only thick, but also efficiently soundproofed. A deafening wall of sound hits us. Two huge cylinders spin side by side in a pit wide and deep enough to hold an automobile. Thankfully, a safety barrier surrounds the machine. The grinders spin slowly, but their mechanized teeth are frighteningly large. All in all, an injection seems preferable right now.

The goons start heading out. They may be locking us in, but at least they haven't killed us. Suddenly, Jackie slams her handcuffed wrists against the wall. Before I finish saying to myself that she's lost it, the cuffs spring open.

She lunges at one of the goons and drives the open cuff into his carotid. He collapses, grasping his throat. In a flash, Buffy grabs his head and twists sharply, snapping his neck.

As the other goon moves to grab her, Jackie jabs her makeshift weapon into his face. He lets out an excruciating scream and blood spurts from his face. She's poked his eye out. Gross!

Jackie finishes him off in exactly the same way as his buddy. She comes over, grabs my wrists and rams them against the wall. The handcuffs fall to the floor. I can't believe it.

"French model. Stamped Manurhin 2003. Defective. The laughing stock of the small-arms world. Grab a gun." I do so. Jackie takes the other guy's gun and his security card. I feel like kissing her, and something tells me she wouldn't protest, but for now we sprint back toward the laboratory.

§ § §

The guards forced Eytan to sit down. Overwhelmed by painful memories, he didn't have the strength to resist. This place was nothing like the laboratory where he underwent such torture over sixty years earlier. The room was chillingly modern. The floors and walls were covered with a gray industrial paint. The three beds on either side and the medical equipment made it look like the emergency room of a hospital, an impression reinforced by the paleness of the artificial light. How many "patients" had Bleiberg tortured in here?

Relieved that the monster they had been warned about appeared totally impotent, the guards relaxed for a moment. A half-second too long. Eytan banged his cuffed hands down on the cart carrying the monitoring equipment. Jackie was right. But with one busted shoulder, fighting two fully fit men and an armed woman held no appeal. Eytan needed a bargaining chip.

Before the guards could react, Eytan jumped onto the bed, bounced once and leaped feet first at Bleiberg. Instead of hitting him, Eytan wrapped his calves around his dumbstruck target's head. They crashed onto the floor. Despite the old man frantically lashing out, Eytan wasn't about to loosen his hold.

Elena sized up the situation with disconcerting serenity. On his back, arms and legs thrashing ineffectually, the professor briefly reminded her of a turtle lying helpless on its back. "Get out, and stand guard by the door," she ordered the two guards. "I have to negotiate with Mr. Morg."

They glanced at each other in surprise but gave in to the woman's authority. When they had left, Elena walked toward Eytan and Bleiberg.

"Don't worry, Professor. I'm here."

§ § §

Despite the fatigue cramping his muscles, Eytan tightened his hold. His successful maneuver had won him a hostage, but the sudden jarring movements had accelerated his loss of blood. A more experienced opponent than Bleiberg would have broken free. The temptation to get it over with, to break the monster's neck once and for all, was overwhelming. But in Eytan's diminished state, a hostage would be crucial.

A few paces from the incongruous couple entwined on the floor, Elena began to applaud. "Agent Morg has lived up to his flattering reputation. What daring, what brilliance. All with one shoulder out of commission."

"Stop there." Eytan's command lacked assurance, but Elena obeyed, holding her arms wide as a sign of nonaggression.

"OK, look, I've stopped. Tell me, Eytan, I'm curious to know what you hope to achieve, exactly. Save your friends or force me to destroy the facility in order to sabotage our plans? If that's the case, I fear your hopes will be dashed. You can no longer stop the Project."

She drew her gun and pointed it at the two men. Bleiberg tried to speak, but the windpipe, compressed by his creation's powerful thighs, emitted only gurgling and hissing sounds.

Elena's dark eyes locked onto Eytan's. "You've been fighting unworthy opponents for too long now, my friend. The ability to make decisions and act on them without being inhibited by moral standards decreed by cowards is no longer considered an asset these days. Now people trade off. Compromise is the golden rule. Force is stigmatized. Once upon a time, you knew the real meaning of power. But over the years, an insidious evil has possessed you—compassion."

She leveled her gun at Eytan. Then suddenly lowered her hand a fraction. Two gunshots later, Professor Bleiberg breathed his last, his heart and head pierced by two perfectly aimed bullets. The Israeli agent had released his hold and rolled away just before Elena opened fire.

"That's the hostage variable eliminated from the equation. Now everything is much simpler. Stand up. And don't pull the cripple trick. You don't need any help."

His legs as stiff as tree trunks, Eytan struggled to his feet and stood as upright as his strength would allow. He glared at his enemy. In her eyes, he saw the end of a journey that he had been forced to begin sixty-eight years earlier.

CHAPTER 39

One gunshot rang out. Eytan fell back as the bullet perforated his right thigh. Flat on his back, he tried to push himself up with his left arm. Muscles straining, he made it halfway, but the pain was too intense.

He slumped back down.

Elena Kourilyenko walked over languidly, savoring the grimace disfiguring the giant's face. "I have dreamed of killing you for so long, brother. You can't imagine the honor you do me. Eytan Morg is a legend in our organization. Our messiah has a name: Subject 302. Your exceptional talents have made our greatest projects possible. They made me possible, too. I see surprise in your eyes. Don't you understand? You showed the way, but somebody had to follow."

She raised her sleeve, revealing a blue-ink tattoo on her forearm: 985. "They modified you?" Eytan mumbled between gasps for breath.

The young woman stood over him, gun aimed between his eyes. "Modified, no. Perfected! I volunteered, brother. I knew the risks and rewards of the experiment. And I had faith."

"You're mad." Eytan's eyes were filled with profound and genuine distress.

"No. Far from it. You and I represent the greatest leap forward in the evolution of our species. We guide humanity toward the next stage of its existence. I would have liked walking alongside you, but you are so weak. I cannot establish a new order by glorifying weakness. You understand, I hope."

"I understand that it's crucial to stop you and destroy all traces of the Bleiberg Project."

Elena hunkered down, pressing her knee on his wounded thigh. Eytan screamed as his blood began to pump out.

"The only trace that will be destroyed is your colossally failed existence. We could have achieved so much if you hadn't turned against your masters."

She pressed the muzzle of her gun against his sweating brow. Eytan's features relaxed. A smile spread across his face. He burst out laughing. His demented cackle echoed around the laboratory, surprising and irritating his assassin. She pressed harder on his thigh.

A slender finger pulled the trigger. The fatal shot was fired...

§ § §

Jackie and I sprint breathlessly down the deserted hallways. We could have escaped—anybody with any sense would have gotten the hell out of there. But without a word or a moment's hesitation, we head straight for the laboratory. These sickos may have killed Eytan already, but if we have even the slightest chance of rescuing him, we have to give it a try.

We reach the final intersection, turn right and nearly collide with two guards standing outside the double doors. Before anybody can draw a gun, a knock-'em-down, drag-'em-out battle ensues.

I'm no fighter, but I don't like taking shit without giving any back. The guy's well trained. I dodge or parry his kicks with my forearms. Each block hurts more than the last. He forces me back step by step, with no chance to counter. Given our size difference, I must have twenty-five pounds on him. If I can just connect, I'll send him flying. But he keeps coming relentlessly. I'm dripping in sweat. It trickles down my face. My shirt sticks to my skin. With my luck, I'm going to die of dehydration.

I won't give up. I won't give in. I thought the fight went out of me months ago, after I killed that infant. I abandoned my mother and disappointed Bernard. But I won't let Eytan down. C'mon, you bastard, give me all you got. I deserve it.

My back hits the wall. A flurry of punches rains down on me. I protect myself as best I can. A jab to the ribs drops me to my knees. I gasp for breath. The guy steps in to finish it off. He grabs me. I see his feet in front of me, wide apart, and seize my opportunity. I lunge forward and grasp and twist his balls. He screams and lets go of me. I squeeze as hard as I can, with every ounce of my anger. His mouth is wide open, no sound coming out and no air going in. I'm enjoying this. I give him an extra twist and watch his reaction.

His expression is pathetic, ridiculous, lips puckered, eyes bulging. I push with my legs as hard as I can. He topples backward, but I go with him, refusing to let go. I crawl over his body and smash my fists into him. All I can hear are my grunts and his groans. I would have liked hearing him scream, begging me to spare his life, but he's in no state to give me that gratification. I batter him until my fists are numb. All I can feel is indescribable pleasure. In the depths of my brain, I hear a sound repeating itself over and over, getting louder. My name. Jackie...

I spin round. Buffy's in trouble. I don't know how it happened, but the guy's behind her, clutching her neck with his left hand. The douchebag's ramming her head against the wall. Her face is covered in blood, her legs are wilting. He's gonna kill her. I jump up as fast as I can.

No time to think. I sprint and dive at him from behind. Years of college gridiron come flooding back as I hit him with a perfect tackle, crunching into his kidneys. Caught by surprise, he smashes headfirst into the wall. The sound of bones snapping leaves no doubt about it—nose and jaw are broken outright. I find myself slumped over the unconscious scumbag. Jackie collapses next to me. She has a cut over her eye and bruised cheeks and lips. She's spent. With one trembling hand, she passes me the swipe card, stammering, "I'm fine. Go! He needs you!" Eytan...

I draw my gun, but it's purely psychological—I've never used one in my life. I swipe the scanner by the door and enter. Bleiberg's body lies in a pool of blood. Elena isn't far away, squatting over my buddy, a gun pointed at his head. He lets out a bloodcurdling scream. The redhead hasn't noticed my entrance. I creep forward. Payback time.

§ § §

Eytan felt the bullet graze his temple. The gun dropped to the floor, and Elena's mouth pressed against his ear as her full weight crashed down on him. She let out little high-pitched squeals, then straightened up abruptly.

Her hands scrabbled at Jeremy's forearm as he gripped her neck in a viselike stranglehold, pulling back with all his strength, cursing and spitting out his hatred of the woman. The force of his hold bruised her flesh, which went from pink to crimson to purple. One more tiny effort and her spine would snap in two.

§ § §

The bitch hasn't heard me approaching. Tough shit. I get a good firm grip, strangling her with my one arm and ramming a knee into her back. As I pull back with all my might, she has no chance of escape. And I'm savoring her groans. Despite the effort, I grin maniacally. You killed my mother and Bernard, and I bet you took care of my father. Three excellent reasons to snuff you out, like Eytan would, without a hint of remorse.

I feel her resistance weakening. All I have to do is keep pressing with all my strength to snap her in two in cold blood. And become like them, like her. But I've already killed. By my own stupid recklessness. By killing her, I will take another irrevocable step and abandon all hope of ever finding peace one day. The infant girl would become merely the first victim in the process of my degeneration. So, no, I won't kill Elena.

I'll let others dispense justice or play God.

§ § §

Jeremy released his hold and backed up. Gasping for breath and coughing, Elena fell to the floor, her hands clasping her inflamed neck. Eytan grabbed her gun and the hand Jeremy held out to pull him up. Trying to find the least painful position, the giant leaned heavily on the young guy's muscular shoulder.

Jeremy's expression was serene. Eytan saw a glimmer of pleasure in his eyes.

"You did right. She's not worth dirtying your hands. Killing her wouldn't relieve your pain, but it would take away any chance of getting a normal life back. You're not a killer, Jeremy."

The trader's eyes flitted from Eytan to Elena. "I know that now."

The redhead spoke up. "You are a killer, Morg. We made you. Your fine words won't change that. You are Subject 30…"

Before she could finish, a kick in the face from Eytan knocked her out cold. "I am not the product of an experiment. I belong to nobody but myself. Bleiberg could change people's bodies, not their minds. Nobody dictates what I do. I am the captain of my soul."

He turned to Jeremy. They gazed at the professor and the hit woman, stretched out side by side. "Do you understand now why I do this job? I give the victims the justice they deserve."

"Wouldn't it be better to protect them before they become victims?"

Eytan looked down and took a deep breath. "For that to happen, man would have to stop being a wolf. Meantime, I decimate the pack."

The giant glanced toward Jackie, who was propped against the lab's double doors. Her face bore the scars of combat, but the spectacular wounds would heal without a trace. The petite blonde observed the scene in silence. She stared at Eytan and hobbled toward them. When she reached Jeremy, who couldn't take his eyes off Elena Kourilyenko, she murmured, "Jeremy, it's time to go."

The trader glanced at his companions. Smiled. "Too right. I've had more than enough of this. For a ragtag bunch, we didn't do too bad. What happens next?" His wry grin faded when he saw their serious expressions. "What's wrong?"

Looking him straight in the eye, Eytan replied, "The Bleiberg Project must end here and now. This facility must disappear."

"Of course!"

"Along with everything that has anything to do with that psychopath." Eytan nodded toward Elena, still out cold on the floor.

Jeremy was about to nod but stopped as he realized the true meaning of Eytan's words. Blind panic washed over his face. "No, Eytan! You don't have to do that. Let's blow up the lab and the whole complex, then we can go home. Please, quit fooling around."

Morg grasped Jeremy's shoulders. "As long as I'm alive, they will hunt me down. If they capture me, the research will start again. My body would be their holy grail. It's true what Bleiberg and Elena said. I am Subject 302. For the Consortium, I always will be."

Jeremy shrugged off Eytan's hands. The giant's wounds and precarious balance prevented him from resisting. Seething with anger, the trader moved toward Jackie, who still hadn't spoken. "Make him see sense. It doesn't have to end this way. It can't end this way." The CIA agent held Jeremy's gaze but didn't utter a word.

"You're both absolutely crazy, goddammit! Do you have to be stupid to be a secret agent or what?" He glanced at Jackie. "Isn't there a witness protection program that gives you a new identity and everything?"

"Can you see me living in a sleepy suburb, working nine to five as a pen pusher at city hall or in a government office?" asked Eytan. "I'm a hit man, Jeremy. I never learned to do anything else. I'm tired. My job is done. Others can take over. Now help Jacqueline, and get out of here as fast as you can, both of you."

"No way!"

Jeremy didn't see it coming. Eytan winced as his fist crunched into Jeremy's jaw, but the punch had enough power to deck him.

"Jackie, looks like it's up to you to haul him out."

"What are you going to do?"

"I think you have a vague idea."

Rising onto her tiptoes, Jackie gave the giant a kiss on the cheek.

§ § §

I come around in the car with Jackie leaning over me. Her slender fingers caress my face. I sit up. He certainly gave me one hell of a punch. I can hardly move. The car starts up. As we drive away, I stare at the ruins of the racecourse buildings in the side mirror. A first explosion sends heaps of earth flying. A series of blasts, each more powerful than the last, engulfs everything in flames. Eytan always did things thoroughly.

Hands clenching the wheel, Jackie stares at the road ahead. We drive in silence. I'm going to miss the bastard.

EPILOGUE

Snow piles up in the driveway. I'm going to have to get the shovel out if I want to make it to work tomorrow morning. The kids, at least, will have some fun, because it looks like there won't be any school. Cup of coffee in hand, I gaze across the road. Colorful Christmas decorations light up every house. I'd better not forget. My wife's aunt and uncle fly into Newark tomorrow evening. I have to pick them up at seven.

I'm pleased to be out of Manhattan. Smalltown, New Jersey, suits me much better. The air is pure; the people are friendly. I've made more friends in five months than in five years in NYC. I don't miss the world of finance. Running a bookstore is more fun. I've named it Morg's World. I sell crime fiction, thrillers, espionage novels and some role-playing games. Who cares if it doesn't make a cent. We have enough money not to worry about that. The store has a few aficionados already. Some stop by every day. We chat over a pot of coffee. We fight. We make up. Life is back to normal. I no longer see the world through columns of numbers.

I quit drinking. When we got back from Belgium, I had a short stay at a rehab center. Ever since, the mere sight of a glass of wine turns my stomach. I still smoke, but less than before. I can't quit completely.

I still have trouble sleeping, but it's gradually getting better. I make the most of it to catch up on my reading and fill the gaps in my general knowledge. That'll take some doing. Often, at night, I wonder what Eytan's life was like after he escaped the concentration camp. How did he dodge the Nazis and survive? Who supplied him with antidote? A whole host of questions, to which I'll never have an answer. I can't help thinking of the guy, an extraordinary eyewitness to history in the making, and all he went through.

Once a week, I visit my mother's grave. Before she resigned from the Agency, Jackie arranged for a reburial in the local cemetery.

She thought it wiser not to inform her bosses of the Consortium's existence. I wanted to expose the whole thing, but she pointed out that the evidence went up in the explosions at the BCI facility in Belgium. According to Jackie, the shady organization wouldn't hurt us, because we are no longer a threat. As she said, "Who'd believe us anyway?"

I can't deny she's right. Nobody has come to assassinate us. As for the influenza epidemic, it was successfully brought under control within a few weeks of our return home.

A quick glance at my e-mails before bed. The desk is piled high with books. I'll never be able to read all of them, but trying won't hurt. Three new messages. Two online orders—more parcels to gift wrap—and one whose subject line reads *Merry Christmas, Novacek.* A chill runs down my spine. I never use that name. It can't be spam. If it's a virus, Greg, the fat geek who virtually lives in the store and on Facebook, will take the machine apart and put it back together.

I click, and it launches an animation that starts with a photo of the store. I can see myself through the window, chatting with a bearded guy, Phil. It was yesterday afternoon. The image fades and is replaced by a message: *Merry Christmas to both of you!*

Another image comes up. Two fists close-up. Letters on the knuckles: Y-O-U-R M-A-T-E.

The bastard! A hand lands on my shoulder. I'm not startled. I'd recognize her touch anywhere.

"You knew, didn't you?"

"Yes. I get the feeling Eytan Morg has a new target. Life's going to get tricky for the Consortium."

She nuzzles my neck and whispers in my ear.

"Merry Christmas, sweetheart."

Thank you for reading The Bleiberg Project.

We invite you to share your thoughts and reactions on Goodreads and your favorite social media and retail platforms.

We appreciate your support.

ABOUT THE AUTHOR

David Khara studied law, worked as a reporter for Agence France Press, was a top-level athlete, and ran his own business for a number of years. Now he is a full-time writer. Khara wrote his first novel—a vampire thriller—in 2010, before starting his Consortium thriller series. The first in the series, *The Bleiberg Project*, became an immediate bestseller in France, catapulting Khara into the ranks of the country's top thriller writers.

About the Translator

Simon John was born in the United Kingdom. After graduating from Cambridge University, a quest for wine, women and goat cheese led him to Paris, where he began working in film production and translation. He primarily translates and subtitles movies, such as Michael Haneke's Palme d'Or-winner *Love* and blockbusters *Taken 1 & 2*. After twenty fertile years and 3,713 goat cheese salads in Paris, he is now based in Berlin.

About Le French Book

Le French Book is a New York-based digital-first publisher specializing in great reads from France. It was founded in December 2011 because, as founder Anne Trager says, "I couldn't stand it anymore. There are just too many good books not reaching a broader audience. There is a very vibrant, creative culture in France, and the recent explosion in e-reader ownership provides a perfect medium to introduce readers to some of these fantastic French authors."

www.lefrenchbook.com

DISCOVER MORE BOOKS FROM

LE FRENCH BOOK

The 7th Woman by Frédérique Molay
An edge-of-your-seat mystery set in Paris, where beautiful sounding names surround ugly crimes that have Chief of Police Nico Sirsky and his team on tenterhooks.
www.the7thwoman.com

The Paris Lawyer by Sylvie Granotier
A psychological thriller set between the sophisticated corridors of Paris and a small backwater in central France, where rolling hills and quiet country life hide dark secrets.
www.theparislawyer.com

The Greenland Breach by Bernard Besson
The Arctic ice caps are breaking up. Europe and the East Coast of the United States brace for a tidal wave. A team of freelance spies face a merciless war for control of discoveries that will change the future of humanity.
www.thegreenlandbreach.com

The Winemaker Detective Series by Jean-Pierre Alaux and Noël Balen
A total Epicurean immersion in French countryside and gourmet attitude with two expert winemakers turned amateur sleuths gumshoeing around wine country. Already translated: *Treachery in Bordeaux, Grand Cru Heist* and *Nightmare in Burgundy*.
www.thewinemakerdetective.com

CPSIA information can be obtained at www.ICGtesting.com
Printed in the USA
BVOW11s1220030614

355222BV00004B/5/P